The Sluts

Also by Dennis Cooper

The George Miles Cycle:

Closer (1989)

Frisk (1991)

Try (1994)

Guide (1997)

Period (2000)

God Jr. (2005)

My Loose Thread (2002)

Wrong: Stories (1992)

The Dream Police: Selected Poems '69–'93 (1994)

Violence, News Item, Literature (2004)

All Ears: Essays, Cultural Criticism, and Obituaries (1999)

Collaboration:

Dennis (2004)

Weird Little Boy (1997)

Horror Hospital Unplugged (1997)

Jerk (1993)

The Sluts

Dennis Cooper

New York

Dennis Cooper is very grateful to Don Weise, Alex Kasavin, Todd James, Hooboy's male4malescorts.com, Yury Smirnov, Joel Westendorf, and Ira Silverberg.

Pieces of *The Sluts* first appeared in the magazines *Blackbook*, *The Prague Literary Journal*, Nerve.com, and *Sebastian*, and in the anthologies *Frozen Tears II* (Article Press) and *Full Frontal Fiction: The Best of Nerve.com* (Three Rivers Press).

Hachette Books
Hachette Book Group
1290 Avenue of the Americas
New York, NY 10104
HachetteBooks.com
Twitter.com/HachetteBooks
Instagram.com/HachetteBooks

Previously published by Carroll & Graff in 2005.

First Hachette Books Edition: 2023

Published by Hachette Books, an imprint of Perseus Books, LLC, a subsidiary of Hachette Book Group, Inc. The Hachette Books name and logo are trademarks of the Hachette Book Group.

Print book interior design by Sue Canavan

Library of Congress Cataloging-in-Publication Data is available.

ISBN: 9780786716746 (trade paperback)

Printed in the United States of America

LSC-C

Printing 22, 2026

Contents

Site 1

Review #1

Escort's name: Brad

Location: Long Beach

Age: 18?

Month and year of your date: June 2001

Where did you find him? Street

Internet address: no

Escort's email address: none

Escort's advertised phone number: not advertised, but try 310-837-6112

Rates: I gave him $200

Did he live up to his physical description?

Did he live up to what he promised?

Height: 5′11″?

Weight: 150 lbs.?

Facial hair: no

Body hair: pubes only

Hair color: blond (dyed)
Eye color: hazel
Dick size: 6 inches?
Cut or uncut: cut
Thickness: couldn't tell
Does he smoke? yes
Top, bottom, versatile: bottom
In calls/out calls/not sure: not sure
Kisser: yes
Has he been reviewed before? no
Rating: recommended (see review)
Hire again: no (see review)
Handle: bigman60
Submissions: this is my seventh review
URL for pics: no

Experience: There are usually a few street hustlers working the blocks around a local bar here in Long Beach called Pumpers. That's where they like to hang out and play pool between tricks. It's a pretty sad scene, so I couldn't believe my eyes when I saw this beautiful, skinny kid with a backpack who told me his name was Brad. He didn't look a day over fourteen, but his ID said 18 so I'll let it stand at that.

I took him back to my place. He was very quiet and didn't seem to want to talk. He wouldn't give me a price or say what he was into. He also had a slight twitch where he'd crane his neck and open his mouth. I took that to be a drug reaction since he was obviously on something. There were warning signs everywhere but Brad was so hot that I just ignored them. I'm glad I did, but keep reading.

He asked if I had any alcohol. I thought he was high enough already, but he said he had to be 'fucked up to do it.' So I gave him some whiskey and he proceeded to get quite drunk but not loud and obnoxious. If anything he got even quieter. He still wouldn't talk money or specifics. He gave me the impression that whatever I wanted to do and pay him was fine. After about thirty minutes of steady drinking, I decided to make a move.

Here's the thing. The sex was unbelievable. Brad will do anything as far I can tell, but he's definitely a bottom. He never got hard, but he sure acted like he was into it. He has the hottest, sweetest little ass, especially if you like them a little used like I do. I must have eaten out his hole for an hour. I got four fingers inside him. I couldn't fuck him hard and deep enough. I spanked him, and not softly either. I pinched and twisted the hell out of his nipples. Nothing fazed him. All the time his cute boy face looked at me with his mouth wide open and made these sounds like he was scared to death and turned on at the same time. I came twice, first in his mouth and then up his ass. I should say that I never practice unsafe sex, but I just couldn't help it. I'm HIV-, however.

Here's where the problems started. He didn't want to stop. It's like he couldn't get himself out of whatever zone he was in. I was afraid he'd lost his mind. It was very spooky. I didn't know what to do with him. I let him sleep over because he didn't seem dangerous, but I fell asleep to the sound of him whimpering and thrashing around. I left $200 for him on the dresser, and when I woke up, he and the money were gone. There was a note from him with his phone number on it saying to please call him or tell my friends about him. Overall, it was great, but once is enough for me.

You: I'm a middle-aged, overweight top into teenaged street trade, the cuter and skinnier the better.

Review #2

Escort's name: Brad
Location: Long Beach
Age: 18 (LOL)
Month and year of your date: June 2001
Where did you him? on this site
Escort's advertised phone number: 310-837-6112
Rates: whatever you want to pay him. I gave him $150
Did he live up to his physical description: yes!
Did he live up to what he promised: fuck, yes
Height: 5'9"?

Weight: 145 lbs?
Facial hair: no
Body hair: no
Hair color: blond
Eye color: green
Dick size: don't care
Cut or uncut: don't care
Thickness: don't care
Does he smoke? yes
Top, bottom, versatile: bottom
In calls/out calls/not sure: out
Kisser? don't care
Rating: what do you think?
Hire again? fuck, yes
Handle: llbean
Submissions: this is my first review

Experience: The earlier review of Brad seemed too good to be true, but I called him anyway. It turned out to be the phone number of a homeless shelter in Long Beach. I left a message for Brad not expecting to hear back, but he called me a few hours later. He sounded unfriendly and bored on the phone, but I told him what I was into and he said that was fine. I offered to call him a taxi, but he said he wanted to walk. It must have been a good ten mile walk to my house from that location, so I figured right then that he was a little strange. He arrived maybe two and a half hours later. I opened the door and couldn't believe my eyes. He seriously looks about fourteen, and they don't get any cuter.

Brad looked and smelled like he hadn't showered for a while, but from the earlier review I'd expected as much. I personally like my boys a little lived in. I met him at the door with a bottle of Jack Daniels, and he just took off the cap, and chugged about half of it down while I stripped him. He has a very tight, adolescent looking body with long, skinny arms and legs, and the smallest ass and about twelve pubic hairs. The earlier review stated Brad was spooky, and he has some mental problems for sure, but I'm not into being some kid's father, so I could care less.

I don't have the space to go into everything we did, so I'll cut to the chase. Brad let me handcuff him to my bed and I went to work on his ass. I gave him a good finger stretching then started burying bigger and bigger dildos in his ass. I got a fat, two foot long dildo all the way inside and he let me churn and pound that ass like I was making butter. The whole time, he screamed like he was dying, but his dick was always rock hard. When I finally got around to fisting him, his hole was so hot that I came within a minute, then sucked the sweetest, biggest load of come out of him that I've ever tasted.

It was clear that he could have gone on all night if I'd wanted. I did have to order him to leave, and he was very out of it and acting pretty strange. But let me tell you, he's worth it. I'll be hiring him again for sure.

You: Leather daddy type, mid-50s, into restraints and heavy anal sex with young looking bottoms.

Review #3

Escort's name: Brad
Location: Long Beach
Age: 18?
Month and year of date: July 2001
Where did you find him: on this site
Rates: not applicable
Height: 5′9″
Weight: 130 lbs.
Facial hair: no
Body hair: no
Hair color: brown
Eye color: blue
Dick size: don't know
Cut or uncut: don't know
Thickness: don't know
Does he smoke? yes
Top, bottom, versatile? don't know
Rating: not applicable
Hire again: not applicable
Handle: JoseR72

Submissions: This is my seventeenth review

Experience: Call me a caretaker if you want, but after reading Brad's reviews, I couldn't help but feel concerned about this troubled young man, and angered by the callousness with which the previous reviewers have treated him. I work in the mental heath industry in Orange County, not far from Long Beach. I made an appointment with Brad in order to encourage him to seek treatment, although he didn't know my intentions until we met.

Regular visitors to this site know that I'm not against hiring escorts. I will even admit that Brad is my type and that meeting him involved a high degree of self-control on my part. Something the previous reviewers are right about is that he's extraordinarily cute. Brad is one of the cutest twinks I've ever seen in fact. I don't know how a boy as cute and young as Brad ended up in the low end of his profession, but it's wrong to exploit him. He deserves better.

I had a long talk with Brad. It took him a while to open up to me, but he did. My knee-jerk diagnosis is that Brad is probably schizophrenic with an untreated chemical imbalance. He might also be suffering from a mild neurological disorder, as evidenced by the physical tics that the first reviewer mentioned. He allowed me to drive him to the facility where I work and enroll him in an outpatient program. I set him up to live at the home of a female acquaintance of mine. He is no longer at the phone number posted here and with any luck, you have heard the last of him. Shame on you.

You: Hispanic male in my late 30s.

Brad responds: Don't believe this guy. He's a prick. I have a new number. It's 310-666-9876. Call me if you're a generous man. I'm up for anything. I need a place to live too. This guy's a fucking prick. I don't need help. He's a liar. I'm writing this on his computer. What does that tell you? Guys like him are the worst. They promise you shit and they don't mean it. Don't call me if you're like him.

Webmaster's message: My repeated attempts to contact JoseR72 and have him confirm this review have been unsuccessful. Until further notice, I strongly advise all of you to stay clear of Brad.

Review #4

Escort's name: Brad
Location: Los Angeles
Age: 18
Month and year of your date: July 2001
Where did you find him: this site

Escort's advertised phone number: pager 310-666-9876
Rates: $500 overnight
Did he live up to his physical description: yes
Did he live up to what he promised: no
Height: 5′10″
Weight: 130 lbs
Facial hair: no
Body hair: pubes
Hair color: dirty blond
Eye color: hazel
Dick size: 6 inches
Cut or uncut: cut
Thickness: less than medium
Does he smoke? not with me
Top, bottom, versatile? total bottom
In calls/out calls/not sure: Out with me
Kisser: yes
Rating: not recommended
Hire again: no
Handle: bizeeb7

Experience: I read the warning on Brad, but I was in the LA area on business and decided to take a chance. I called the number expecting a pager but Brad answered. Despite what has been said about him, he was quite talkative, too talkative if anything. I suspected he was on drugs at the time, but in retrospect I think he was in the manic phase of whatever mental illness he is suffering from. I offered to pay for his taxi ride to my hotel near the LAX airport, and he said he wasn't far away and would leave immediately. I waited for him in front of the hotel for more than two hours, then gave up and went to sleep after trying to reach him by phone with no luck.

At about 3:30 in the morning I was woken up by a call from the lobby saying a young man was here to see me. I asked the concierge if there was a taxi waiting, and he told me there was. I asked him to pay the driver and charge it to my bill and send the young man up to my room. Big mistake. When I let Brad in, he was in a very agitated state. He wanted alcohol but I told him there was none in the room, and that room service was closed. He seemed extremely upset by this and sat on the bed and began crying. I was half-asleep, naked, frightened, and wondering what the hell I'd gotten myself into. I suggested that we go try to find an open liquor store, but he said no. I offered to call him a taxi and even pay him the full, agreed upon amount if he wanted to leave, but that just made him even more upset. He started saying, 'Don't you like me,' and things like that, which I have to admit I found rather heartbreaking.

I didn't know what to do, but I told Brad that he could go ahead and get undressed and that we'd give sex a shot. I really wasn't in the mood, but I thought he might be carrying a knife or something, so it was more of a safety precaution at that point. When I said that, he calmed right down, and took his clothes off, and even made a few jokes about how crazy he'd been acting. Like the other viewers said, Brad is an extremely cute boy. Without his clothes on, he took my breath away, if it weren't for his height, I'd guess from his body he was no older than thirteen or fourteen. He has a slim, slight build with tiny nipples and the most precious little ass. It was just too arousing, and I decided that I had to indulge myself a little.

Brad didn't so much suck my cock as open his mouth and let me pound his throat as deep and hard as I wanted. Previous reviewers mentioned Brad's poor hygiene, and while he certainly wasn't the cleanest escort I've ever been with, he smelled and tasted like a boy should. Rimming him seemed to drive both of us out of our minds. As soon as I started eating his hole, he had almost what seemed like a seizure. His whole body spasmed violently, and his mouth opened wide, and his eyes rolled back in his head. It sounds frightening, and it was, but it was also incredibly hot to see a boy that cute lose control. I knew from the earlier reviews that Brad could be barebacked, and that's a huge fantasy of mine, so I fucked him condom-free and had two orgasms inside him before I felt too exhausted to continue. Still, I was dying to taste his come. He was still seizing and shaking all over, so I jerked him off and felched his hole until he shot, then licked up his delicious load.

As soon as Brad came, his seizure seemed to come to an end. He was drenched in sweat, and looked disoriented and exhausted. I suggested we get some sleep, as I was very spent by that point. That's when things suddenly went bad very fast. Brad started yelling and screaming at the top of lungs that I was a sicko who'd had unsafe sex with him against his will. He was out of control, and soon enough there was a loud knock at my door. It was the hotel's manager and a couple of employees. He took one look at us and told me to either get the boy out of the hotel immediately or I would have to leave. I asked him to call Brad a taxi and that I would have the boy downstairs ready to leave in a minute, and he agreed and left. (God knows what would have happened if the manager hadn't been gay!) Brad continued to scream at me, one minute saying he was sorry and to please let him stay, and the next minute telling me he was going to tell the police I raped and tried to kill him. I just kept begging him to get dressed and leave, and he finally did, but not before calling me every terrible name in the book.

The nightmare didn't end there. About a half an hour later he started calling my cell phone, begging me to come get him, and that he didn't know where he was, and that he was scared. I tried to reason with him, but he got more and more upset, threatening to kill himself. He told me there was someone who wanted to kill him, and that if I didn't come get him, he was going to go over to this person's house and let himself be killed, and that he didn't want to die, but he was afraid he would do that if I didn't stop him. After about five calls from Brad, I turned my phone off. I don't know if he's alive or dead, or if he was just trying to fuck with my head. I've never had anything like this happen to me in all my years of hiring escorts, and I thought I should warn others interested in Brad that, as cute as he is, he is definitely not worth it.

You: Asian-American man in my early 30s, like to try new things, into young guys, generally a top.

Review #5

Escort's name: Brad
Location: Los Angeles
Age: let's just say 18
Month and year of your date: ongoing
Where did you find him: here
Internet address: bdax@hotmail.com
Escort's email address: bridax@hotmail.com
Escort's advertised phone number: 310-655-0033
Rates: Available on request
Did he live up to his physical description? if you hurry
Did he live up what he promised? and more
Height: 5'10 1\2"
Weight: currently 150 lbs.
Facial hair: no

Body hair: no
Hair color: dishwater blond
Eye color: aquamarine
Dick size: 6 inches
Cut or uncut: cut
Thickness: medium
Does he smoke? not anymore
Top, bottom, versatile? bottom
In calls/out calls/not sure: In or out
Kisser: depends
Rating: highest
Hire again: ongoing
Handle: brian
Submissions: This is my first
URL for pics: no

Experience: I read with great interest the most recent review on Brad. I believe I'm the man Brad mentioned who "wants to kill him." Let me explain something to you all. Both of my parents died of brain tumors. After reading the first three reviews of Brad, I was convinced that his physical and behavioral problems were the result of an undiagnosed brain tumor. I arranged a date with him, but instead of bringing him back to my place for sex, I took him to a hospital and paid for him to have a series of tests to see if I was right. It turns out that Brad does have an advanced, inoperable brain tumor and will die from complications resulting from the tumor within the next six months. That night I moved him into my house and he has been living here off and on for the past few weeks. I am paying for all of his medical bills, as well as his day to day expenses. He is on a medication that greatly reduces the severity and frequency of his seizures, although the side effects cause him to be very fatigued and irritable. For two days earlier this week, Brad went off his medication and disappeared, and this is when and how the previous reviewer had the date with Brad that he described. Brad is now home and on his medication again and doing as well as could be expected.

Before you decide that I'm a saint, I should explain that my all time fantasy is to murder a boy during the sex act. I've had sex with a number of boys who were perfectly willing to be killed, but something always stopped me from going all the way. Brad provides me with the ideal situation, and, except for our disagreement earlier this week, he is also sexually aroused by what we both have agreed will happen. If all of this seems hard to believe, maybe it would help to know that in addition to his fatal condition, Brad suffers from severe bipolar disorder. He grew up in foster homes and has been emotionally, physically, and sexually abused his entire life. He will tell you himself that since he moved in with me, he has felt security and contentment for the first time.

When the day comes that he is so disabled that sex with him is no longer exciting to either one of us, I am going to end his suffering. In the meantime, I will allow him to do escort work on a limited basis. Anyone interested in seeing Brad can email or phone me, and arrangements will be made.

You: none of your business

Webmaster's comments: On July 16, reviewer JoseP72 was found severely beaten in his apartment. He remains in a coma. While there is no evidence to suggest that Brad is responsible, I nonetheless urge you to stay away from Brad. However, due to your overwhelming interest in the Brad saga, I will continue to post any reviews and updates that come in. Let me also say that because "Brian" has never posted on this site before, and because a new review of Brad that I will post in the morning throws the veracity of "Brian's" post into question, his claims should be taken with a grain of salt.

Review #6

Escort's name: Brad aka Steve
Location: Long Beach
Age: 20?
Months and year of your date: July, 2001
Where did you find him? Pumpers
Rates: $400
Did he live up to his physical description?

Did he live up to what he promised? yes
Height: roughly 6 feet
Weight: maybe 165 lbs.
Facial hair: no
Body hair: pubes, ass crack
Hair color: brown
Eye color: blue
Dick size: 7 inches
Cut or uncut: cut
Thickness: medium thick
Does he smoke? like a chimney
Top, bottom, versatile: top for rimming only
In calls/out calls/not sure: out
Kisser: no
Rating: overpriced
Hire again: maybe
Handle: baglover
Submissions: This is my third review

Experience: Not that the Brad story needs another wrinkle, but here's mine. I hired "Brad" about three weeks ago. I question how much of what the two previous reviewers wrote is true. I suspect the reviews were written by Brad/Steve himself. I went looking for Brad at Pumpers in Long Beach after reading the first review. It turns out that I'd seen him there a number of times drinking and sometimes playing pool or pinball. I had been told by the bartender that his name was

Steve. He stood out because of how young he looks, but apart from being cuter than your usual street trade, I wouldn't say there was anything supernatural about his appearance. He had a reputation among the regulars at the bar as an arrogant creep who charged a ridiculously large fee ($350) to sit on men's faces and masturbate. That was the extent of his services, and even getting him to agree to that meant buying him many drinks and waiting until he was in the mood, which could take hours. Need I say that this "Brad" is a very different character from the boy described in the recent reviews? The only things that match are his young appearance and the facial tics and body twitching that everyone describes.

I had a couple of drinks and decided to ask this character if he was Brad. He looked shocked but he said he used that name sometimes. I explained that I'd seen a review of him on this site. He said he knew nothing about the site, and had never even used a computer much less surfed the web. I used his curiosity to get him to agree to go home with me, telling him I'd show him the review on my computer. Maybe I caught him off guard because he seemed like a nice enough boy at the time and even agreed to let me top him. But after a few more drinks, he started acting in what I would call a bizarre and aggressive manner. He changed his mind about coming to my place and insisted we go back to his place instead, which I agreed to. It was hardly a homeless shelter. It was quite a pricey, upscale apartment an hour north in Los Angeles. Let me say for the record that there was no sign that anyone else lived there, so it wasn't the home of the self-styled murderer Brian. (He also had a very expensive G4 computer in full view, but he didn't seem to care that I'd caught him in a lie.)

As soon as we arrived, he became very cold and matter of fact. He told me to sit on the couch then pulled his pants down and sat on my face. I rimmed him for a few minutes until he came. I hadn't come yet, since I was expecting to top him, but he refused to continue, although for an additional $50 he did agree to sit on my face for another couple of minutes. I will say that if your fantasy is to rim a decent looking piece of jailbait, he's quite satisfactory. He has a delicious, baby soft ass with a talented hole that he genuinely seems to enjoy having eaten, but whether it's worth the money is up to you. Clearly what the previous reviewers wrote about Brad is a bunch of lies and nonsense. BTW, he still hangs out at Pumpers. I saw him there two nights ago.

You: Good looking, early 30's, keep myself in shape. I'm a top who loves to rim young guys.

Brian responds: While Brad is in no condition to respond personally at the moment, I'm almost sure I know this lying asshole. First of all, if I'm right, it was my condo. I was there in the room watching the entire encounter. Brad had just moved in with me the day before, and he was at Pumpers only to tell some old friends there about his diagnosis and say goodbye. Brad says this guy badgered him for sex the whole time he was there. He finally agreed and brought the guy back to the condo. Brad has always been a bottom who will accomodate any scene for a price. This guy offered Brad $300 dollars to rim him. That was his request. Brad accomodated him. During the scene, he decided that he wanted to eat shit out of Brad's ass, which cost him an additional $100. He also drank Brad's piss for no extra charge. Since that night he has hounded me, asking to come over and eat Brad's shit, and on three occasions we accomodated him. He's obsessed with Brad, and ultimately I found his constant phone calls and emails tiresome and stopped accomodating him. This is undoubtedly the reason that he has chosen to lie about Brad. Even his physical description of Brad has no resemblance to the reality. This guy is just an ugly, fat pedophile and scat queen who got his heart broken. End of story. Let me add that Brad is available as a WS, scat, body fluid top or bottom if you're interested.

Review #7

Escort's name: Kevin aka Brad
Location: San Diego
Age: 22

Month and year of your date:
Where did you find him? Boys-Next-Door Agency
Rates:
Did he live up to his physical description?
Did he live up to what he promised?
Height: 5′9″?
Weight: 135 lbs?
Facial hair: no
Body hair: don't know
Hair color: blond
Eye color: hazel
Dick size: about 7″
Cut or uncut: cut
Thickness: don't remember
Does he smoke? he used to
Top, bottom, versatile: bottom
In calls/out calls/not sure:
Kisser: used to
Rating:
Hire again:
Handle: cuteystevieinsd
Submissions:

Experience: A friend of mine told me about this site. I wish it were around a couple of years ago when I was doing escort work full time. Maybe some of you old timers (LOL) remember me as Stevie of San Diego. I worked mostly through The Boys-Next-Door Agency. I also starred in a whole bunch of porn videos under the name Stevie Sexed. I'm a website designer now, but I have good memories of those days. A big hug to all those generous men who helped me out back then. Any of my old regulars who want to say hi can email me at cuteystevieinsd@earthlink.net. Hey, business is a little slow right now, so you never know (smile).

I'm writing because of this whole Brad thing going on here. When I knew Brad, he used to call himself Kevin. He was with Boys-Next-Door for a while. I called Ed at Boys-Next-Door, and I think he's going to post something here too. I'm 99.9% sure this is the same guy. I worked with Kevin as a duo a few times, and he used to tell me he had a secret plan to become the most famous escort in the world. I think the guy Brian is the same man who was Kevin's sugar daddy back then. I can't tell you much more about him, but I remember he was a first rate creep.

If I'm right, and I like I said I'm 99.9% sure I am, then this whole thing is a big scam by Kevin. I can tell you that Kevin would be about twenty-two by now, although he looks a lot younger. He told me his parents are rich and that he grew up in La Jolla. He's obsessed with serial killers like Jeffrey Dahmer and claimed to me that he was offered a million dollars to be in a snuff movie, and that he was being paid to procure boys to be in snuff movies by some rich guy in LA. It was complete bullshit. He was a lying, phony rip off artist, and I'm sure he still is. Don't be fooled.

You: Cute blond boy, 24 but look much younger, 5'8", 130 lbs., uncut, great ass and legs, versatile but prefer bottom, affectionate, intelligent, and likes the company of older, generous men.

Brian responds: What can I say? I don't know this little lying twerp and neither does Brad. Brad never worked for any agency. He never lived in San Diego. Like I told you before, he grew up in a series of foster homes in Texas and Oklahoma. Let me add that if Stevie is the same Stevie Sexed who appeared in a number of porn videos a couple of years back, then I'm interested to learn that he's still alive, since I remember reading an article in Frontiers Magazine about HIV+ porn stars that stated Stevie Sexed was on his death bed with advanced AIDS-related pneumocystis. These new AIDS drugs are a miracle, aren't they? His old "regulars" might want to ask for a current photo before throwing good money at this sick, lying, has-been bitch. Note to Stevie: You were pretty cute and hot back in the day. If you feel like going out with a bang, give me a call (smile).

A message from Ed at Boys-Next-Door Agency: First I want to thank all the guys who've posted such glowing reports on Boys-Next-Door and our escorts. We're grateful for your business, and I hope that shows in the quality of our service. I really don't know if this Brad is Kevin who worked for us briefly nine months ago. I have posted pictures of Kevin on the Hall of Fame page on our site. Maybe that will help solve the mystery. Kevin was let go over concerns about his true age and for no other reason. I don't recall having met anyone named Brian and I have no knowledge of Kevin having had a sugar daddy. As to Stevie's claims, he is a bright young man whom I grew quite fond of during the time that he worked for us. So it pains me to say that complications from his ongoing battle with AIDS have taken a toll on his mental state. I advise our loyal Boys-Next-Door customers that any dealings with Stevie should be carried out with caution.

Review #8

Escort's name: Brad
Location: Los Angeles
Age: 18
Month and year of your date: July 2001
Where did you find him: chat room
Internet address: no
Escort's email address: bradsucks@hotmail.com
Escort's advertised phone number: don't know
Rates: $800/3 hours
Did he live up to his physical description? no
Did he live up to what he promised? yes

Height: 5′10″
Weight: maybe 150 lbs
Facial hair: no
Body hair: no
Hair color: blond
Eye color: green
Dick size: 6 inches
Cut or uncut: cut
Thickness: nice
Does he smoke? not with me
Top, bottom, versatile: bottom!!!
In calls/out calls/not sure: in with me
Kisser: don't know
Rating: Wow
Hire again: in the works
Handle: secretlifer34
Submissions: This is my first review

Experience: I found Brad in a chat room, knowing nothing about the thread about him on this site at the time. He described himself as a cute twink and hungry assed bottom into heavy use and abuse. I told him I was an S&M top into bondage and he gave me a price of $800 for the evening. I thought that was steep, but he said he was extremely good looking and a pig and well worth it, so I agreed. I drove over to his place since he said he only does In calls.

When he met me at the door, I was a little disappointed. He

has a beautiful face but is quite delicate looking and slightly fem, which is not my usual type. But after a few minutes of talking with him, and looking at that innocent, adorable face I was horny enough to go through with the scene. I'd asked him to wear clothes he didn't need anymore, and he was wearing an old t-shirt and holey jeans through which I could see hints of his completely hairless and porcelain looking legs and ass. Whether he was my type or not, they looked very vulnerable and ripe for a nice hard whipping.

We had a beer and got to know one another. That's when he told me about the controversy raging around him on this site. He was hyper and talked too much about himself and a lot it didn't make a whole bunch of sense, but that made me want to dominate him even more. When I put the duct tape over his mouth and that queeny voice was out of the picture, it was about as hot as it gets. I could see a nice hard on in his jeans, so I held him by the shoulders kneed him in the balls harder and harder until he was retching and couldn't stand up but was still hard as a rock.

I'd paid for the whole evening, so I took my time. I ripped his clothes off and spent about two hours working him over. I'd brought an arsenal of dildos, and his ass gobbled up every last one of them. I left the biggest one inside him and whipped his back and ass and legs very hard, and used a stun gun on his groin until tears and snot were running down his face. I couldn't believe a kid that slight could take that kind of pain. After some heavy tit torture and CBT, and a heavy whipping of his chest, stomach, and thighs, I couldn't hold it in any longer and practically drowned his face with the biggest load I've ever shot in my life.

Afterwards when I was paying him he got needy on me. It was about 5 am and I was ready to leave. After I use a guy, I'm bored and contemptuous and Brad was really working my nerves with his begging me to stay and keep going or take him home with me. I admit I lost it and punched him in the face, but even lying on the floor with blood running out his nose and a split lip he wanted more abuse. It was too much for me at that moment, and I had to get out of there. But the next day I couldn't get him out of my mind, and I'm thinking of making arrangements for him to come over tonight and give it up in my playroom.

About all the reviews of Brad: Some of it rings true, but a lot of it doesn't. I saw no roommate. He had a tattoo of Christ's face on right upper back that one else has mentioned. He was a queeny chatterbox and didn't drink or seem drunk when I got there. He's a skinny kid but he doesn't look sick to me. Is he mentally ill? I would say yes. Also I should say that I visited the Boys-Next-Door website and he looks nothing like Kevin. It's not the same guy. Hope that helps.

You: White, late 40s, a little overweight, very dominate S&M top who likes to take a cute young stud to his limits.

Brian responds: This never happened. Either this review is a fraud or some escort is passing himself off as Brad. Not that Brad wouldn't be up for a scene was heavy as the one described here, he would. But it would cost you a fuck of a lot more than $800 and Brad is very weak so there are limits to how active he would be in such a scene.

Stevie responds: I'm not going to get into a war of truths with anyone but I just want to say that Kevin from Boys-Next-Door had a tattoo of Christ on his upper back and everything else the reviewer says about Brad sounds exactly like Kevin. It makes you wonder, doesn't it? Also thanks to all you great guys who've sent me well wishing emails. The truth is I was sick for a while but I'm totally fine now and look as good as I ever did. I think Ed's just pissed off with me because I wouldn't sleep with him but I'm very professional and don't think it's cool to sleep with my boss. I am taking clients again. Just email me and we'll set it up and thanks again to everyone who cares about me.

Review #9

Escort's name: Brad
Location: Beverly Hills
Age: 18
Month and year of your date: July 2001

Where did you find him? email address
Escort's email address: bradsucks@hotmail.com
Rates: not relevant
Rating: A++++++
Hire again: not relevant
Handle: secretlifer34
Submissions: This is my second review

Experience: I know you have a policy against posting more than one review of an escort, but maybe you'll make an exception under the circumstances? I had my second date with Brad. He called me from a payphone out of the blue and asked if he could he come over. I was glad to hear from him, and gave him directions to my house. He insists he is Brad, and that the house where we had our first date was Brian's house, and that Brian was watching us through a two-way mirror. He said that Brian just likes to play games with the guys who look at this website. He showed me three bottles of pills that he says he takes to control the seizures caused by his brain tumor. It seemed important to him that I believe his story, and I would say that I do think my Brad is probably the Brad everyone is writing about, but I don't think it matters anymore.

When I opened my front door, he looked much more damaged than I remembered, which he explained as the result of a fight he'd had with Brian on the previous night. He had a very swollen black eye, and one of his ears was caked with dried blood, and his left wrist was very swollen and obviously broken. I could tell he was in a lot of pain, so I offered him some valium. He took five of them and asked if he could lie down and rest for a minute. I told him that was fine as long as he stripped first, so he did, and stretched out on my couch.

Someone (Brian?) had really done a number of Brad, and I admit to feeling quite jealous. There were big, dark bruises, whip marks, and what looked like cigarette burns on his chest, back, upper arms, thighs, and crotch which had been shaved and apparently either scalded or burned by some kind of chemical. I asked him what happened and he said that Brian had started to kill him but chickened out at the last minute, and that's when they fought. I'll admit that I was about as titillated as I've ever been, but I had a pang of conscience and tried to talk Brad into reporting Brian to the police. He said it didn't matter since he was going to die soon anyway, and he'd rather die like this than in a hospital. When he said that, he gave me the coldest look I've ever seen, and it was very clear to me what it meant.

I don't expect anyone reading this to understand what happened next. I'll just say that we had a talk and then he asked to use my phone to "call Brian" and see if he would agree to what we'd decided. I put that in quotes because the call Brad made was obviously a fake. I could hear the voice on the other end saying, "At the tone the time will be . . ." over and over. It was bizarre. Brad "talked to Brian" about what he and I had discussed then told me that "Brian" had said it was okay if I transferred $20,000 dollars into his account. First of all, I don't have that kind of money to spare, not to mention that it was after banking hours so I couldn't have arranged the transaction even if I did have the money. All I could think to do was offer to transfer the money in the morning, so Brad asked "Brian" if that was okay, and "Brian" agreed. The strangest thing of all was that Brad really seemed to believe he was talking to someone on the phone. Either that or he deserves an Academy Award. I still can't decide whether he's a complete nut case, or really is losing his mind on account of a brain tumor, or if it was all part of some brilliant suicidal scheme. I think the pure craziness of it all is what made go ahead and play along with it.

I don't know how to talk about what happened. I know I shouldn't go into it for a lot of reasons, but I think I need to talk about it for the sake of my sanity. Brad is the heaviest masochist I've ever met, heard about, or even imagined in my fantasies. I cut him with a knife and whipped and beat his whole body until there was nothing I could do would stop the bleeding. I broke his nose and jaw and may have accidentally broken his neck. I squirted lighter fluid on his genitals and ass and lit them on fire a couple of times. I was so into it that I thought he died about halfway through the scene, but he didn't. After what I just said, this will sound ridiculous, but when I realized he wasn't dead, I couldn't bring myself to go through with it. He's in my playroom right now screaming for me to kill him. I've gone in there several times with a gun planning to blow his brains out, but I couldn't. I keep giving him valiums to try to ease his agony, but I don't think it helps very much. I honestly don't know what to do except wait for him to die from his injuries. Any suggestions would be very welcome.

You: already told you

Brian responds: First I have to make a confession. When I wrote that the encounter between secretlifer34 and Brad never happened I was lying. I won't explain my reasons here, but just know that I'm telling the truth now. The review posted by secretlifer34 was full of lies and deceit. I don't even know where to begin. Brad does not have a tattoo of any kind on his body. He's not queeny, and you'd have to be blind not to know he's ill. This guy did pay $800 to do a very rough scene with Brad, but he went way too far and I had to order him to leave. Brad is very unwell boy with severe physical and psychological problems. Secretlifer34 is a sick individual who got off on taking advantage of Brad's vulnerabilities. He also showed unforgivable disrespect to me and to my relationship with Brad. It's true that there was a physical fight between Brad and myself, and that Brad has run away from home like he has done before on several occasions. While I don't believe a word this evil individual and pathological liar has to say, and suspect he is playing a mind game on me for his own sadistic pleasure, I ask that if Brad is by some remote chance staying with him, or if he or anyone reading this has knowledge of Brad's whereabouts, that you do the right thing and either bring Brad home immediately or inform me of Brad's whereabouts so I can collect him. Regardless of what any of you think of me, Brad and I are in a relationship as sacred as any marriage. I'm asking for your help for my sake and for Brad's. I will offer a substantial reward for Brad's safe return. Name your price, just please please please help me out.

Webmaster's message: I have reason to believe that Stevie of San Diego not only wrote this review as well as many of the other reviews, but is also "Brian." I can't prove that, but based on some information that I have just received from a source that I consider to be reliable, it is a very strong suspicion. If anyone has a legitimate review of Brad, please post it. Otherwise, I will continue to try to separate the fact from the fiction, if there are any facts to be found. Stay tuned.

Review #10

Escort's name: Stevie (Brad?)
Location: San Diego
Age: 18?

Month and year of your date:

Where did you find him?

Internet address:

Escort's email address:

Escort's advertised phone number:

Rates:

Did he live up to his physical description?

Did he live up to what he promised?

Height: 5'6"?

Weight: 130 lbs?

Facial hair: no

Body hair: crotch, armpits

Hair color: brown

Eye color: blue I think

Dick size: about 7 inches

Cut or uncut: uncut

Thickness: thin

Does he smoke? no

Top, bottom, versatile: versatile bottom

In calls/out calls/not sure: not sure

Kisser: yes

Rating:

Hire again?

Handle: corey4escortsd

Submissions: only this one

Experience: Maybe I can help clear up this Brad bullshit.

Excuse my French. :-) I'm a San Diego based escort. My professional name is Corey. I've been reviewed on your site as Corey #3. A few weeks ago I was hired to do a three-way with a client and a second escort named Brad who I was told would play the bottom for the client and myself. When I arrived at the client's house, I realized the bottom was Stevie. I knew Stevie from when we both worked for Boys-Next-Door. I'd heard through the grapevine that Stevie was having some problems with his health, so I told the client that I wouldn't top Stevie without wearing a condom. Since I was hired for a bareback scene, he was pissed off at first but finally agreed. The scene went fine and we both topped Stevie. I'll give him credit for being a great bottom. I'm hung 9" and thick and the client was even bigger and we double fucked him with no problem at all. Afterwards Stevie and I shared a cab home since we both live in the same part of town. I told him I'd heard rumors about his health and asked how he was doing. He said he was in bad shape and didn't think he'd be around much longer. He said he was turning tricks to pay off doctor bills but his main thing was that he was looking for someone to kill him in a snuff video. I'm not kidding. He said that if I knew anyone who was interested, I should tell them to email him. He said he'd always wanted to be famous. He thought that was the only way left for him to be famous now. He also told me (and this why I'm writing) that he'd taken the name Brad as part of a scheme had to get some guy named Brian who posts messages on this website to kill him in a snuff video. I didn't even know about this website when he told me that, believe it or not. He also told me that there was an escort named Kevin who'd worked at Boys-Next-Door and gotten killed in a snuff video. He said he'd seen the video and that's what gave him the idea. He said an ex-lover had shown it to him. He said he'd stolen it and now his ex-lover was trying to destroy his reputation by lying about him on this website. He didn't tell me the ex-lover's name but I'll try to find out and tell you all. He asked if I wanted to come over and see the video. I definitely did not want to do that at the time, but now that I know about the whole Brad and Brian thing on your website (everyone's talking about it by the way) I decided I should go for it. I always wanted to be a spy! :-) I'm going over to Stevie's place on Sunday afternoon to check it out. A friend of mine told me that for my own safety I should put this whole thing out there so everyone will know and Stevie won't try any weird shit on me. I'll let you know.

You: Gorgeous, hunky top, 24, 6 feet, 185 lbs, blond, blue eyes, hung, bubble butt.

Webmaster's message: I have spoken with Corey and confirmed that this is an authentic email. Of course Corey's story itself cannot be confirmed. Regarding the existence of this snuff video, all I can report is that Ed from Boys-Next-Door reiterated that there was an escort named Kevin who worked for the agency fifteen months ago. He was fired and subsequently went missing. He said the period of Kevin's employment was so brief that he has no record of the escort's address or phone number. Also, I'd like to repeat that if anyone has hired the Brad described in Brian's posts, please submit your review. I'm asking for a legitimate review from a reliable source only.

Review #11

Escort's name: Brad?
Location: Beverly Hills
Age: 18?
Month and year of your date: August 2001
Where did you find him? where I left him
Height: 5′10″
Weight: 160 lbs?
Facial hair: no
Body hair: no
Hair color: blond
Eye color: hard to tell
Dick size:
Cut or uncut:
Thickness:
Does he smoke?

Top, bottom, versatile? no category
Rating: off the chart
Hire again: no
Handle: secretlifer34
Submissions: This is my third review

Experience: I just want to report that Brad (or whoever) passed away this morning at 4:27 am. After my last review, I was contacted by a man who I will call Rex. He said he would help me out and kill Brad for a certain fee. I agreed to meet him at a bar, and once I was convinced he wasn't law enforcement, we drove to my house. I don't want to say too much about Rex for the obvious reasons, but he has appeared in several widely available S&M videos and I recognized him straight away. On the drive home I asked him if he'd killed before, and he said he had, but only as part of a "group effort," as he called it. He said he'd been paid a lot of money to take part in two snuff videos. He said the first time he'd been very morally conflicted and did it because he had huge credit card debts. But he said it was hotter than any sex he'd had, so the second time he did it as much for pleasure as for the money. He asked me if I knew who Chip Noll the porn star was. I told him that I owned a few of Chip Noll's videos and had even tried to hire him about a year before when he was doing escort work but had been stood up. Rex then told me Chip Noll had been snuffed in the second video. So if you ever wondered what happened to him, there's your answer.

I asked Rex what it was like, and he said that when he arrived Noll was already naked, heavily drugged, and sitting in a big metal washtub. Rex said he and Noll had been in an S&M video together and dated a couple of times so it was a weird situation. He said there were two other men and they were each given a task to carry out, and that the whole thing took less than an hour. He said one of them poured boiling water over Noll's body while he and the third man mutilated Noll's face, chest, and genitals with scalpels until he eventually died from loss of blood. Rex said Noll got a hard on as soon as they started and stayed hard, and that the only way they knew he was dead was when his dick got soft. Rex said Noll lived an amazingly long time, and that his face looked like something out of a horror movie quite a while before he died. He said they were all so turned on by killing Noll that after the camera was turned off they snorted a bunch of crystal meth and carried Noll's corpse over to this mattress and gang raped it. Anyway, there you go. When we got home and I took Rex into see Brad, I think he was really disappointed and kind of repulsed by how far gone Brad was. I guess I'd gotten used to how he looked. Rex looked at Brad for a minute and said he was just going to put him out of his misery, then leaned over and strangled him to death very quickly. I don't know what I thought it would be like, but I started crying from exhaustion and just the whole thing. Rex was very understanding and helped me dismember the body and told me about a safe place to get rid of it. The only other thing I have to tell you is that Rex looked at the bottles of medication Brad had with him and said that they were definitely drugs to treat seizures. So I think this might be the end of the Brad story.

You: I told you

Webmaster's message: Like secretlifer34's previous two reviews, this one should probably be considered part of a prank. Email sent to his address was returned and hotmail.com has no record of an account under that username.

Review #12

Escort's name: Renn
Location: Los Angeles
Age: 42
Month and year of your date: August, 2001
Where did you find? Clients call me
Internet address: www.rennadams.org
Escort's advertised phone number: 917-691-5705
Rates: $350 hour, $2500 overnight
Did he live up to his physical description? count on it
Did he live up what he promised? count on it
Height: 6'3"

Weight: 230 lbs.
Facial hair: moustache
Body hair: shaved
Hair color: salt and pepper
Eye color: brown
Dick size: 10 x 61/2
Cut or uncut: uncut
Thickness: thick
Does he smoke? cigars
Top, bottom, versatile: top
In calls/out calls/not sure: In or out
Kisser: no
Has he been reviewed here before: yes
Rating: guaranteed best ever
Hire again: they always do
Handle: rennadams
Submissions: no
URL for pics: www.rennadams.org

Experience: I think I'm the person referred to as Rex in the pack of lies passing for a review that was posted here yesterday. I don't mind people creating a little controversy and fun, but not at the expense of my reputation and livelihood. The truth is I was hired by a guy to do an S&M top scene with his boyfriend. It's true he wanted to meet at a bar first so we did. We discussed terms there, then I followed him in my car to his house. I've been a recovering drug addict for eight years and I did not drink or use drugs on this or any other occasion. Other than looking seriously under-aged, the boyfriend did not have more than a few marks on him at that time. I said I couldn't proceed with the scene without proof that the boyfriend was of legal age. The guy who hired me produced a driver's license that put the boyfriend's age at eighteen, if he was eighteen then I'm the Queen of England, but it's not my place to decide if a piece of identification is real or not, so I proceeded with the scene I was hired to do. I was never formally introduced to the boyfriend, and no names were used during the scene, but the driver's license had first his name as Brad.

The boyfriend took a good amount of pain and abuse to his body and face. It was a hot scene that I enjoyed a whole hell of a lot, but at no time was the boyfriend's life in any danger during the three hours that I was there. Anyone who's employed my services or watched my videos knows that I'm an expert at doling out abuse and taking bottoms to their limits without crossing the line. I was told to make verbal threats against the boyfriend's life throughout the scene, but it was never anything more than fantasy role play from my point of view. If something happened to the boyfriend after I left, it's not my responsibility and I know nothing about it. Why this guy has chosen to exaggerate our activities in anyone's guess. I just wanted to make clear what really happened.

You: rennadams

Webmaster's message: After speaking with Renn Adams on the phone, I believe he is telling the truth. Based on certain details that he passed along to me in private, I question earlier reports that Stevie is the mastermind behind the Brian and Brad saga. If the experience Renn describes here involved Brian and Brad, I ask that the strangely silent of late Brian confirm Renn's review.

Review #13

Escort's name: Steven aka Stevie (aka Brad?)
Location: San Diego
Age: early 20s
Month and year of your date: August 2001
Where did you find him? online
Internet address: no
Escort's email address: cuteystevieinsd@aol.com
Escort's advertised phone number:
Rates: $350 for three hours
Did he live up to his physical description? no
Did he live up to what he promised? yes
Height: 5'8"
Weight: 115 lbs?
Facial hair: no
Body hair: no

Hair color: brown
Eye color: brown
Dick size: 6 inches
Cut or uncut: uncut
Thickness: no
Does he smoke? no
Top, bottom, versatile? bottom
In calls/out calls/not sure: out with me
Kisser: yes
Rating: not sure
Hire again: no
Handle: bigred
Submissions: This is my sixth

Experience: With the confusion about Stevie and Brad, I'll post this review of Stevie here since it seems to relate. I was one of Stevie's regulars when he worked at the Boys-Next-Door Agency. We hadn't hooked up in over a year so I was surprised to get an instant message from him asking if I wanted to get together. I have a freakishly large penis (14") and it's rare that I find a bottom willing to accomodate me, especially since I'm an aggressive, marathon top man into small, thin, boyish types. Stevie could take a deep, hard pounding all night long. His retirement from the escort business had delivered a serious blow to my sex life, so I was thrilled to hear from him and quickly set up a date.

I'd always known Stevie was HIV+. I am too, and all that

meant was bareback sex was no problem for him. I didn't know he'd developed full blown AIDS since I'd last seen him. I must have looked startled by his appearance because he apologized that he'd been ill, and said this was the first time he'd gotten out of bed in two weeks. He assured me that he'd showered and douched before leaving his place, and I was so horny that it would have taken a lot more than a boney face to soften my cock at that moment.

Stevie knows I'm not much for small talk. Once I'd reassured him about his appearance, he stripped, knelt before me, and went down on my cock like the slut he'd always been. He was noticeably thin, and seemed a little frail but it just made him look even younger, and his ass was as pretty as ever. While he gave me head, I leaned over and slapped his ass cheeks until they were flushed and hot. Then I pushed him down his back, threw his legs over his head, and started chowing down on that unbelievable asshole. I didn't realize how much I'd missed it. I've had teenaged tail all over the world and Stevie's ass is in a category all by itself. His years as a heavy bottom have damaged it beyond repair, but you could say the same thing about the Grand Canyon. In looks, smell, and taste, it's one of the true Wonders of the World. I recommend doing him with the lights on because you can stretch the elastic and look all the way into his beautiful, pulsing guts. I sucked and chewed that hole until my jaws were sore, then gave it a fierce, jackhammer fucking until I climaxed twice inside him.

Afterwards I admit that I felt a little guilty because all that activity made him very sick. He was sweating and too weak to stand up and so pale he looked dead. Looking at him lying there like that, I saw death and realized I'd never see him again. I can't believe that perfect ass is going to be dead and rotting away in the ground. I don't mean to be morbid. It's just a huge, huge loss.

You: A tall, average looking white guy in his late 30s with a giant dick and a taste for rice.

Stevie responds: First I want to thank my old pal Red for his review. It's nice to be appreciated. I also want to say that the thing about me writing all of those reviews about Brad is not true. I'm just trying to make a living under terrible circumstances. I don't want to die. I'd do anything not to die. Because of all these lies you've been posting about me, all the sick freaks in the world have been emailing and calling me. My life is hard enough without all of that. I'll do escort work for as long as I can, but I beg you to stop printing these lying things about me. I was unable to keep my graphic design job because of my heath, and I'm now escorting full time. If you're in or traveling to the San Diego area and not a weirdo, please write or call me.

Webmaster's message: I offer my sincere apologies to Stevie for jumping to the conclusion that he wrote the earlier reviews. While their author or authors remain a mystery, there is no evidence to suggest that Stevie is behind them. However, I cannot in good conscience discount the reports made here about Stevie by Corey and Ed from Boys-Next-Door. I therefore urge caution in any dealings with him. That said, I wish Stevie the very best of luck. Also, you should know that I now question the veracity of the information I received from escort Renn Adams. A good friend of Adams's who is also a trusted contributor to this site has informed me that Adams admitted he was involved in a scene that went too far. This contributor says that Adams has cut off contact with his friends and regulars, and his current whereabouts are unknown. Lastly, I also want to say that this thread of reviews about Brad has drifted far away from the matter at hand and this concerns me. While the controversy around Brad has greatly increased the amount of traffic on this site, complaints about it are also mounting. I would ask that we all try to stick the goal of reviewing Brad. Otherwise, I may be forced to eliminate this thread from the site. This is your first and last warning.

Review #14

Escort's name: Brad
Location: Marin County
Age: unknown (claims to be 14)
Month and year of your date: September 2001

Where did you find him? Hitchhiking
Internet address: unknown
Escort's email address: unknown
Escort's advertised phone number: unknown
Rates: $200
Did he live up to his physical description? doesn't apply
Did he live up to what he promised? yes
Height: 5′9″?
Weight: 155 lbs.?
Facial hair: no
Body hair: no
Hair color: light brown
Eye color: hazel?
Dick size: unknown
Cut or uncut: unknown
Thickness: unknown
Does he smoke? yes
Top, bottom, versatile: bottom?
In calls/out calls/not sure: not sure
Kisser: no
Has he been reviewed before? I think so
Rating: good
Hire again: no
Handle: ticktock88
Submissions: none before
URL for pics: no

Experience: I can't be absolutely sure, but I think I had sex with Brad about a week ago. I live in the northern part of Marin County, but I make bi-weekly business trips to San Francisco. I was driving home one morning from one of these trips when I saw a boy hitchhiking. A lot of hippie-type people live in the area where I'm from, and it's not so unusual to see hitchhikers. I occasionally will pick them up if I'm in the right mood, or if they're really cute. This hitchhiker looked adorable and not your usual hippie-type, so I offered him a ride, which he accepted.

Up close, I could see that he'd been in a recent fight or something, as he had black eye and some cuts and bruises on his face. I asked him about them, and he said his dad had beaten him up and he was running away from home. I asked him why his dad beat him up, and he said it was because he told his dad he was gay. I told him I was gay, and we had a good talk about the difficulties of being gay in this world. He seemed like quite an intelligent and sweet young man. To cut to the chase, he said he had no money, and that if I would loan him some, he'd show me 'a really good time,' in his words. I was really quite smitten with him by then, so we agreed on $200, and I pulled off into a rest stop.

We had sex in the back seat of my car. There wasn't a whole to it due to the cramped quarters, but he was a great kisser, and gave me one hell of a blowjob and even swallowed my come without my asking. He said I could fuck him, despite the fact that I didn't have any condoms on me. I was sorely tempted, but he didn't smell so great, and had strong BO, so I declined. It was after we were back on the road that I started to put two and two together. The thing that really made wonder were his physicals tics or little seizures, which seemed to become much more dramatic after the sex was over. I asked him what his name was, and he said Brad. I thought to ask him if he was the same Brad, but considering the kind of scary reviews he's gotten here, I decided to leave it alone. I was going to offer to let him spend the night at my house, but after the sex he became a lot less friendly and talkative. He started answering my questions with sarcastic comments, and at one point even said he wondered what the police would do if he told them I'd had sex with a fourteen year old boy. By the time I got to the turn off to my house, I was relieved to see him go.

The more I think about, the more I'm convinced it was Brad. The physical stuff matches, and my gut feeling tells me that I'm right. If so, he's apparently alive and headed north. If he's Brad, I can tell you that he is one very attractive but very screwed up young man.

You:

Webmaster's message: Gentlemen, I think we might just have our first legitimate review on Brad in some time. After exchanging a few emails with ticktock88, I believe him, and am convinced he did have an encounter with Brad. Wonder of wonders. Stay tuned.

Review #15

Escort's name: Brad/Stevie
Location: Los Angeles
Age: said he was 18
Month and year of your date: September 2001
Where did you find him? here
Escort's email address: cuteystevieinsd@hotmail.com
Escort's advertised phone number: 1-733-543-0070
Rates: said $250/hour
Did he live up to his physical description: never found out
Did he live up to what he promised? no
Height: claimed 5′6″
Weight: claimed 110 lbs.
Facial hair: claimed none
Body hair: claimed none
Hair color: claimed black
Eye color: claimed brown
Dick size: didn't ask
Cut or uncut: didn't ask
Thickness: didn't ask
Does he smoke? don't know
Top, bottom, versatile: claimed to be a bottom
In calls/out calls/not sure: claimed in or out
Kisser: claimed yes
Rating: no show
Hire again: no

Handle: lovesexy
Submissions: This is my twenty-eighth

Experience: I've been following the Brad thread with a morbid fascination. Have you sold the movie rights yet? How about Taylor Hanson as Brad and Tom Cruise as Brian? Seriously, as you regulars know, I'm the secretary for a well known Hollywood agent and I think it would make a great independent film. You regulars also know I'm a big old quasi-pedophile from hell so it probably won't surprise you that the reviews of Stevie got my juices flowing. I'm easily the world's biggest fan of the porn star Stevie Sexed, and the chance to sleep with him was something I just couldn't pass up. I contacted Stevie via email. Apart from insisting that I call him by his 'new name' Brad (!?!), he was sweet and eager to get together. I told him that his health issues weren't a problem as long he looked as cute as he did in his videos. After he sent me an adorable picture of himself, I set up a date at my house and even bought him a round trip plane ticket to Los Angeles. I told him that I wasn't into anything kinky and preferred a nice, simple, affectionate vanilla scene, and he said that was no problem at all. I told him to take a shuttle from the airport to my house and I would reimburse him. He said that was fine. Long story short, he never showed and didn't answer my emails asking what happened. After going back and rereading the reviews and posts on Stevie more carefully, I realize it was screwy of me to expect otherwise. Oh, well.

You: Cuddly overweight queen in my mid-20s who likes to top but thinks kissing and hugging are just as important.

Webmaster's message: I'm very sorry to report that Stevie Sexed was found murdered in his apartment on 8/31/01. According to a report published in the San Diego Union, Stevie (real name Kenneth Miller) had been dead for approximately a week. He was discovered by the manager of his apartment building. The police are investigating Kenneth Miller's murder and I am cooperating with them. At their request, I ask that anyone who had contact with 'Stevie' during the last six months contact the San Diego Police Department. I have received their assurance that no one with information about this case will charged with any crime. You can remain anonymous, and I recommend that you do so. Kenneth Miller is the fifth young man to be found murdered in the San Diego area in the past seven months. The police have reason to believe that these murders are connected. I urge all San Diego based or inbound escorts and customers to use extreme caution until this case is resolved.

Review #16

Escort's name: Brad
Location: Portland, Oregon

Age: 16

Month and year of your date: September 2001

Where did you find him?

Internet address: no

Escort's email address: no

Escort's advertised phone number: no

Rates: doesn't apply

Did he live up to his physical description? yes

Did he live up to what he promised? doesn't apply

Height: 5′11″

Weight: 160 lbs.

Facial hair: no

Body hair: don't know

Hair color: dark blond

Eye color: hazel

Dick size: don't know

Cut or uncut: don't know

Thickness: don't know

Does he smoke? yes

Top, bottom, versatile? doesn't apply

In calls/out calls/not sure: doesn't apply

Kisser: don't know

Rating: doesn't apply

Hire again: doesn't apply

Handle: builtlikeatruck44

Experience: I thought you might be interested in this report, even though it's not technically about a date. I live in Portland, Oregon and run a small home construction business. I've been known to hire the occasional escort. I find this site quite entertaining as well as informational, but I've never posted a review because I prefer to keep my private life to myself.

Four days ago, a young man named Brad showed up at my office asking for a job. I didn't really need anyone, and I don't hire workers who under the age of 18 for a number of reasons, but he seemed like a nice kid, so I offered to pay him under the table if he helped out cleaning up the work sites and running errands for me. I felt kind of sorry for him because he had some kind of nervous disorder that made his right side and face seize up once in a while, although I didn't ask him about that out of politeness.

Brad worked for me until today. He was a hard worker who did help me out quite a bit. He was quiet and didn't really fraternize much with me or the other workers. His girlfriend would drop him off in the mornings, and pick up him at the end of work day. Yesterday her car broke down, and I offered to give him a ride home. On the drive, I had my first extended conversation with him, and this is why I'm writing.

At one point in our conversation, Brad asked me if I was gay. He told me he'd been gay, but was now straight and was planning to marry his girlfriend. He said he'd worked as a prostitute in the LA area, but had quit and moved to Portland because of a bad incident with a man he was living with named Brian. I asked if he was the escort who'd been the subject of all the controversy on this site. He said he knew about this site, but he seemed completely shocked by what I told him. After that, he got very quiet, and we didn't really talk for the rest of the drive.

This morning he showed up at work and told me he was quitting the job, and asked for his last check. He explained that he had looked at this site and read the thread of reviews I'd mentioned. He said the first few reviews were true, but that the rest of them were all lies. He said a john named Brian had offered to be his sugar daddy, and that he had lived with Brian for a while. He said Brian seemed like a really nice guy, and that their sex was kinky but he didn't mind because Brian was very generous, and had even paid for him to start college. He said Brian had pimped him out a few times, and that he didn't like doing that but he felt like he owed Brian.

Brad told me that he had no idea that Brian was writing all these lies about him being sick and wanting to die. He said that one night Brian asked him to have a three-way with another man. He said they all got high, and in the middle of the sex, Brian's friend had gotten violent and beaten him up and tried to kill him, and that Brian was encouraging the friend to kill him. He said Brian was very apologetic afterwards, and blamed the drugs. Brad said he'd believed Brian, but that a couple days later, Brian had tried to kill him, and he'd managed to escape. He said he hid out a friend's place for a week, and then moved to Portland where he'd grown up.

I believed his story. He seemed genuinely angry and upset about what he'd read on this site. I think the fact that I knew about his past as a prostitute made him feel like he couldn't continue to work for me, as he seemed very intent on putting all of that behind and starting a new life. I wish him the best, as he seemed like a very nice young man. Anyway, I thought you might want to know all of that. For the record, he is quite a cute boy, although his physical tics are severe enough that I'd say he's more sympathetic looking than physically attractive.

You: Caucasian, 5'9", 41, solid build, naturally muscular, top, nice guy.

Review #17

Escort's name:
Location:
Age:
Month and year of your date:
Where did you find him?
Internet address:
Escort's email address:
Escort's advertised phone number:
Rates:

Did he live up to his physical description?

Did he live up to what he promised?

Height:

Weight:

Facial hair:

Body hair:

Hair color:

Eye color:

Dick size:

Cut or uncut:

Thickness:

Does he smoke?

Top, bottom, versatile?

In calls/out calls/not sure:

Kisser:

Rating:

Hire again?

Handle: corey4escortsd

Experience: Corey here. I wasn't going to write because I was threatened with bodily harm or worse if I did but I'm quitting the business and moving back to the mid-west in two hours. With Stevie getting murdered I thought people should know about this. I told you I was going over to Stevie's apartment to watch that snuff video he told me about. I did go over there. Stevie said I should show up at 3 o'clock on Sunday but I realized I didn't know where to go. I called

Stevie but he didn't answer his phone or call me back. I decided that he must have meant the address where he'd gotten out of the cab so that's where I went. The door was answered by a blond guy who looked like he was in his early thirties. He introduced himself as Brian and said Stevie had gotten some last minute work but would be back soon. He seemed drunk or maybe high on grass. He offered me a drink but I said no because I definitely didn't trust him. I asked if he was the Brian from this website and he said he was in this calm way that made me believe him. I asked him if Brad was there and he just gave me this really intense look. I felt like he wanted to have sex with me and I kept expecting him to make an offer but he never did in so many words. He told me that he wanted me to empty out my pockets while I waited because he was worried that I was carrying a weapon. So I emptied out my pockets and put everything on a table. I always carry a knife and a canister of mace and I felt nervous without them but by then it was too late and I just wanted to get it over with and get the hell out of there. He told me sit on the couch and wait for Stevie there and he had something he had to do, so I took a seat and he left the room. There were some copies of The Advocate on the coffee table so I started flipping through them but I was too uncomfortable and tense to really concentrate. It must have been about a half hour and Stevie hadn't shown up, so I decided to leave. I gathered up my stuff and was about to go when Brian came back in the room holding a gun. He told me to go sit back down on the couch and wait for Stevie and stop acting like such an asshole. I was totally terrified and thought about trying to mace him but he would have easily shot me before I would have been able to do it. So I sat down and he stood over me with the gun aimed at my head and said if I told anyone about coming over there he would either have me beaten so badly that no one would hire me again or he would kill me himself. I just tried to act really calm and nice and casual, and I said sure, of course, no problem. He looked at me intensely like he was trying to figure something out about me, and then he told me that Stevie was dead. He said if I didn't believe him that he would show me because Stevie's body was in the bedroom, and I told him I believed him but I didn't at the time. I just didn't want to go in the bedroom because I really felt like he was going to kill me. Then he told me that Stevie had been writing to him for weeks saying he was desperate to die in a snuff video and begging for Brian to help. Brian said he came down to San Diego and had sex with Stevie for a couple of days and then murdered him and videotaped it. He asked if I would watch the videotape with him and I told him it would be too heavy for me since I knew Stevie and he said he understood that. I was just desperate to get out there. Then for some reason he seemed to change his mind. He put the gun in his pocket and said I could go, so I took off and until I heard the news that Stevie really was dead, I just thought it was some weird scene that Stevie and Brian had going on over there.

You: see earlier view.

Webmaster's message: I'll be removing this thread from the site and will accept no more postings or reviews on Brad effective now. It seems increasingly clear to me that builtlikeatruck's report on Brad is truthful, and that most of reviews of Brad are fabricated. The contributor to this nonsense who calls himself Brian has just broken his long silence with a review, which I will post in the morning and leave online for twenty-four hours. The police have viewed this email and are considering it a hoax, although they plan to investigate further. Hoax or not, it seems appropriate to let Brian have the last word on this bizarre and troubling saga. For those of you in the Southern California area, you might like to know that there will be a public memorial service for Kenneth (Stevie Sexed) Miller on Saturday, September (8th), 3 pm, at All Saints Church, 532 N. Bedford Street, San Diego.

Review #18

Escort's name: Brad
Location: Los Angeles
Age: better not say
Month and year of your date: 2001
Where did you find him? here

Internet address: no

Escort's email address: it was mine

Escort's advertised phone number: it was mine

Rates: my mind, heart, soul, etc.

Did he live up to his physical description? yes

Did he live up to what he promised? no

Height: 5′10″

Weight: 125 lbs.

Facial hair: no

Body hair: crotch, armpits

Hair color: brown (sometimes dyed blond)

Eye color: hazel

Dick size: about 6″

Cut or uncut: cut

Thickness: medium

Does he smoke? sometimes

Top, bottom, versatile: bottom

In calls/out calls/not sure:

Kisser: yes

Has he been reviewed before? yes

Rating:

Hire again:

Handle: brian

Submissions: some

URL for pics: no

Experience: After reading the recent report that Brad is alive and living in Portland, I've decided it's time to come clean and tell you guys the truth. I'm doing this to clear my conscience, and hopefully to prevent others from being taken in by Brad's act. The truth is I did hire Brad after reading the first few reviews about him on this site. I like skinny, boyish bottoms with an adventurous streak, and Brad sounded perfect. After a night of the wildest, most intense sex I've ever had in my life, I offered to support him financially if he moved in with me, and he agreed. Like I mentioned before, my greatest fantasy is to have sex with a boy and murder him. Brad claimed he found this idea exciting, and told me that when he was with johns, he often fantasized that they were murdering him. He said that in his fantasy, he was dying of a brain tumor and the men were killing him because they couldn't bear the idea of boy as cute as him wasting away in a hospital. Together we came up with the idea of offering the services of "a dying escort" as a way to make our sex life exciting, and because Brad's narcissism needs constant reinforcement. By the way, his physical tics are the result of brain damage from when he was accidentally dropped on his head as a baby. I may be a sick, manipulative, evil man, but Brad makes me seem like Mary Poppins. Living with him was like slowly being driven insane. He's a pathological liar and control freak who has no morality whatsoever. His only goal in life is to be desired and worshipped, and he'll do whatever it takes to addict men to him. He took me to psychological places I should never have gone, and pushed me to do things to him that no one should ever do to another human being. He fucked with my mind, goading me to murder him, flirting with me, begging me to do it, threatening to find someone else to do it if I wouldn't. I think he even half-convinced himself that if I didn't murder him, it would mean he wasn't cute and desirable enough. One night to make me jealous, he talked me into hiring Renn Adams to do an extreme S&M scene with him, and made me watch. Brad is such a egomaniacal, deluded monster that he thinks he has the power to control everyone, but when Brad went too far and told a true, amoral sadist to murder him, he got more than he bargained for. Renn didn't hesitate for a second, and I was so excited that I held Brad down so Renn could finish him off. Brad would have been dead right then if Renn hadn't panicked at the last second about the legal consequences. That night Brad finally pushed me over the edge, and when I saw Renn choking the life out of him, I knew what my life was about. I apologized to Brad and did what was necessary to regain his trust, but from that moment on, his death was all I thought about. Two nights later, believe it or not, he started up again with his 'You should kill me, it would be so hot' number. I just snapped. I walked up behind Brad with a baseball bat when he was watching television and knocked him unconscious with a blow to the head. I dragged his body into the bedroom and raped him, fist fucked him, poured gasoline on him, and went into the other room to get my cigarette lighter. I guess he'd regained consciousness without me knowing it, because when I got back to the bedroom he was gone. At the time, I really thought that Brad might have gone over to secretlifer34's house, since he was a particularly twisted asshole who'd tricked with Brad (and me) one night. But secretlifer34 recently wrote and told me that he fabricated those reviews to get back at me since he was jealous of my relationship with Brad. The fact is, I had no idea whether Brad was alive or dead until builtlikeatruck posted his review, and everything made sense, since Brad is originally from Portland, and it would be just like him to play the innocent straight boy to get what he wanted. The last thing I want to say is that I did not murder Stevie Sexed. I don't know him. I've never been in contact with him. I've never met this Corey person in my life. His review is an attempt either by him or someone else to frame me. If he knew the truth, he'd realize how ridiculous that is. There's a lot more to my relationship with Brad than I can talk about right now, and frankly it's none of your business. For me, the game is over. Right now I just need to think about who I am and what I want and what I've done and what it all means. Best of luck to all of you.

Webmaster's message: An arrest warrant has been issued for David Barrows (aka Corey #3) who is suspected in the murder of Kenneth Miller. The police say there is substantial evidence pointing to Barrows's guilt. They have asked me to urge any of you with information about Corey's recent activities or current whereabouts to contact them. Also, today I received the following update from builtlikeatruck. As he seems to be the only reliable source of information on escort Brad, and since what he has to say is a real eye opener, I'll post it for your interest. Lastly, I've received so many emails asking me not to end this thread of Brad reviews that I've decided to compromise and set up a discussion group for you in the site's Message Center. All future updates that I receive regarding Brad or Stevie's murder investigation will be posted there.

builtlikeatruck's update: I'm afraid I have to make a drastic update and correction on my report on Brad. I appear to have been the latest victim of this young con artist and criminal, but hopefully my actions will make sure I'm the last. Two nights after I posted my last report, I came home to find ten messages on my phone machine from Brad. He sounded very upset, and claimed he'd had a bad fight with his girlfriend. He said he'd gotten her pregnant, and she'd refused to get an abortion. He left a number and asked if I would I call him back. When the phone was answered by the bartender of a very sleazy local gay bar frequented by street hustlers called Rosie's Roost, I should have known. The bartender yelled Brad's name, and he came to the phone. He claimed his girlfriend had thrown him out, and he had nowhere to sleep. He wanted to know if he could crash on my couch for a night. I stupidly agreed, and he showed up about an hour later. As soon as I saw him, I knew I'd made a huge mistake. He was very high on drugs and dressed like your typical street hustler. He was drunk out of his mind, and he reeked of lubricant and semen. He pushed his way into my house, and demanded that I pay for his girlfriend's abortion. When I refused, he started breaking things and threatened to tell the police I'd raped him. I'm not a violent man, but I had to punch him in the face, and literally throw him out of my house. Once I'd locked the door, he started screaming at me from my front yard. One minute he'd say that if I didn't let him in he'd make me sorry, and the next minute he'd beg me to have sex with him and that he didn't care about the money. This went for about half an hour, and he finally left. At about 4 am, I was woken up by a phone call from my foreman telling me that the building where my business is housed was on fire. I drove over there, and, long story short, the building was completely destroyed, and my business along with it. I had no doubt that Brad was responsible. He was arrested yesterday, and has apparently confessed to the crime. He destroyed my life, but at least he'll spend the next few years in prison where he can't hurt anyone but himself. I thought you'd like to know.

Ad

Cute, slim euro trash bottom, 19, 5′10″, 155 lbs, brown hair, blue eyes. Hot, deep butt and mouth. Out only. $250 hr./ $700 overnight. Will do anything for a price. No limits. Email me for pic, more info. at juicyLAboy@ hotmail.com

Hi juicyLAboy, I saw your ad. Sounds good. I'm a total top, 30s, into some kinky and very dangerous shit. I'll pay 5 grand. Send me a nude photo showing your face, ass, and a phone number. We'll talk. Box 157

Hello?

Can I speak to juicyLAboy?

Hi. Box 157, right?

How did you know?

Oh, juicyLAboy isn't my name.

What's your name?

It's Dutch.

You don't sound Dutch.

Thanks.

Okay.

So your email wasn't bullshit?

Was your ad bullshit?

Fuck, no. Oh, this is great. Hi.

Hi.

What's your name?

Brian.

Hi, Brian.

Do you want to explain the 'no limits' thing?

Yeah, um . . . There's just nothing I won't do, I guess.

Nothing?

Not for $5000.

Okay.

I'm strange.

How so?

How so? Because I'm a slut.

It'll be heavy.

Really? I mean I don't care.

Something could go seriously wrong.

Yeah . . . um . . . Oh, I get it.

Go on.

Go on? Okay, um . . . You're very intense.

Extremely.

That's cool, I guess.

So you don't mind if things go seriously wrong.

What? Um . . . I see what you're saying.

Getting cold feet?

No, it's interesting. So I guess you liked my picture.

You're amazing.

Really?

Like you don't know that.

I'm okay. When do you want to do this, now?

Let's say . . . 9 pm tomorrow.

Should I bring anything, or . . . ?

Well, do you have any pictures of you as a kid?

Yeah, I have some. That's funny.

Bring them. Then if something goes wrong, it'll make it more tragic. 'Cos if it goes wrong, it should go really,

really wrong, you know? Like, oh my God, what the fuck have I done?

Okay. Wow, this is . . . Are you going to torture me or something?

To say the least.

You're going to . . . Shit. Okay, no, that's cool.

So you said.

This is great.

Yeah.

I like your sense of humor.

You mean that I have none.

That's great.

Okay.

I have a sick sense of humor too.

I think you're in denial, but that's hot.

You crack me up.

I'd rather crack your skull.

That's great. So can I ask you something, Brian?

Sure.

Are you for real about the money?

Yeah.

You're really going to give me $5000?

Yeah, if you really have no limits, but—

In cash or what?

See, that's funny. You're the one with the great sense of humor. In cash, sure.

Wow.

But I'll have to give it to charity, I guess.

What?

I said I guess I'll have to give it to a charity.

Oh, right. That's funny.

Is it?

Yeah, I mean . . . Oh, right. That's hilarious.

Cute, straight 18 year old white punk rock type with $$$ and heroin problem seeks wealthy man with mansion and drug connection for long term friendship. I like emotional and physical abuse but no sex. Email me for a photo, etc.. Todd Box 631

Todd, Send your photo and a way for me to call you. If I like your looks, you got a deal. Box157

Yeah.

Is this Todd?

Yeah. Frank?

No.

Who is this?

Box 157.

Right. Got it.

It's about the ad.

I know.

I liked the photo.

Yeah. You're calling.

You don't sound interested.

I'm fucked up. So you've got a lot of dope.

As much as you want.

Good shit.

Amazing shit.

Tar?

Tar, rock, powder. You're covered.

Great. Let's do it.

So you look about 5'10", 130 lbs.?

I guess.

And that's a recent picture? You still have the mohawk?

Yeah.

And I can hit you, humiliate you, tie you up. I just want to make that clear. Hello?

Let's do it.

Do you understand what I'm saying?

You do dope?

No.

You should try it.

I did.

Then you should know where I'm coming from.

Where's that? In your words.

Hell.

Hell?

Fuck it, man. Let's do it.

What are you into in bed? Normally. I mean when you're given a choice.

Nothing.

Meaning you don't care?

I don't care, right. Sure.

What about before?

Before?

Before heroin. Before you got into it.

Right. Girls.

You're straight.

Oh, yeah.

But you've been with guys.

No.

Never? Not even for money?

No, man. Come on.

Come on, what?

I was kid.

You were a kid?

Yeah.

You mean when you were a kid . . .

Yeah.

You were abused?

Yeah.

Raped?

What do you mean?

Tell me exactly what happened.

What, or the deal's off?

Let's say yes.

Shit, okay. My uncle . . . did shit to me, okay? Does that do it?

Did what? Under what circumstances?

Fuck. I was staying at his house, and he did shit to me.

Like what?

He did shit to me. What do you think?

Once.

No, a lot.

Against your will.

I was fucking twelve years old. I didn't . . .

Didn't what?

Shit. I liked it, okay? But I was twelve years old.

So what happened to your uncle?

He killed himself.

Why?

Because my parents told the police.

Your parents found out.

I told them.

Why?

Because I was stupid.

You wish you hadn't told them?

What do you fucking think? Shit. Of course I wish I hadn't told them. Jesus fucking Christ.

Oh, okay.

Yeah.

Interesting.

Look, the ad said no sex. I'm not into sex.

Did I say I wanted sex?

Right.

Okay, I do.

I'm not stupid.

It's a test. I think you're really cute and hot. It's a test of my will. And yours.

Fuck.

You're a beautiful kid.

Yeah, whatever.

You are. Don't sell yourself short.

Can't we just do this?

It's really got you by the balls, doesn't it?

What?

Heroin.

Yeah.

So take a cab over here. I'll pay for it.

I can drive.

I'm sure you can, but I want you trapped here. I'll call you a cab. Is now okay?

Whatever, sure.

Cute small Thai boy, 20 but look much young. I like to be the slave for a mean white man who is rich. Bondage, SM,

WS, ff, anything is possible for $$$$. I can be girl or boy. Urgent needing for money to send my family in Thailand. Write to me soon. You ask and I will tell you price. Kwui Chrung Box 119

Kwui. I want to fuck you bareback, shove huge dildos up your ass, and put my fist inside you. I want to fill your stomach with my come and piss. I want to punch you in the stomach until you throw up, then make you lick the vomit off the floor. I want to beat you until you piss and shit and vomit blood. It gets worse. This is not a joke. Name your price. Box157

Dear Box 157, I say very nothing because my English is small. I like be with you as the sex slave. You send $10,000 to Thailand for my family okay? I have no phone use. You come to meet me Jon's Market, 31171 Cadenza Boulevard in Whittier. I work on night. No Sunday. Kwui Chrung Box 119

So you don't mind if I tape record this?

Sorry.

Us talking. You don't mind.

I understand not so much.

Don't worry about it. You're so cute. Look at me. Oh, my fucking God. There is no way in hell you're 20 years old.

I no . . . Sorry.

You're unbelievably cute.

Say again please.

You're beautiful.

Beautiful?

You. You are.

Oh, yes.

I definitely have to kill you.

Sorry?

I'm really high. I'm stoned. I'm fucked up on drugs. You want to get high? You want to smoke some crack?

Drugs, yes.

Here, smoke this. I'll light it.

Ecchh.

More. Smoke some more. That's it. Take another hit. Fry your little brains. That's it.

Oh. I . . . oh.

Okay. And you're going to let me kill you, right?

Yes.

You understand what I mean by that.

Understand? Sorry.

You understand that you're going to die. You.

I . . .

You die. You.

Oh, yes.

You understand. I'm going to kill you. I'm going to rip you apart.

I . . . so sorry.

I kill you. Me. Kill you.

Yes.

Okay, good. When?

When?

When can I kill you? Now? In three hours? Tomorrow? You understand?

Yes. Now.

Now? Right here? In my car?

Yes.

You don't understand what I'm talking about, do you?

Sorry.

Never mind. Let's drive somewhere.

We go?

Yeah.

You send money.

Sure. To whom.

To mother. Sang Chrung.

Okay. Here, hold on a second. Write her name and address there.

Sang . . . Chrung.

Good. Fine. Now the address. Where do you want me to send the money?

Sorry.

Money. Where?

Sorry?

How do I give her the money?

Sorry?

Forget it. Let's go.

Go.

Yeah, go. We're going to drive somewhere, okay?

Go, yes. More drugs please?

Sure. Here. Here's the lighter. Smoke the whole rock if you want. You're so dead.

Sorry?

Dead. You.

Dead?

Exactly.

Dr. Jack Kevorkian type seeks cute, thin 18-24 year old terminal patient type. Anything you want in return, I'll take care of it. Serious replies only. Send photo to Box 157.

Dear Box 157, My name's Wayne. Your ad was weird, but I think I get it. Here's a photo. If you're not a cop, call me. Wayne Box 63

Hello.

Is this Wayne?

This is Wayne.

Hi. It's Box 157.

Who?

Box 157.

Shit.

What?

Nothing. I didn't think you'd call.

You change your mind?

Hardly.

Good.

Mm.

So, why?

Why?

Why did you write me?

I'm just sick of it. I'm just fucking sick of it.

Sick of what?

The whole fucking thing. Everything, everybody. I'm sick of the bullshit. Fucking get up, fucking hang out, fucking go to bed.

I hear you.

Fucking get stoned.

Yeah.

So am I the only one who answered the ad or something?

No, not at all. You're just the one I chose.

Why? Or maybe I don't want to know.

Why do you think?

My looks or whatever.

Exactly. You're like the perfect indie rock grunge boy.

Grunge? That's weird.

I like the long hair, the 'I don't care how I look thing.' You have a very pretty face.

I'm not gay. I don't know if that matters.

It doesn't matter. So tell me about your body.

My body? What do you want to know?

It looks like it would be really nice and skinny. You're tall.

Yeah, I guess.

I hope you're hairless.

Yeah, pretty much.

Even your legs and ass?

Yeah, I guess. Wow, this is pretty weird.

What about your crack?

Shit, I don't know.

Why don't you check and tell me?

Fuck. Yeah, I guess.

No hair.

No. Yeah, no hair. Look, I don't know what to tell you.

So how did you see the ad?

A friend showed me. He thought it was weird.

I guess it is.

Yeah. You're not full of shit, right?

No.

So what happens?

What do you think happens?

I don't know. You said Kevorkian.

Yeah.

So it's like that?

Yeah.

Okay. I don't know what to say. Why do you want to do it, I guess?

I get off on it.

Yeah?

Yeah.

Is it painless?

You want it painless?

Kevorkian puts people to sleep, right?

Yeah.

That sounds okay.

So how old are you?

Eighteen.

Nice.

I'm not gay.

I know. You said. But what does that matter now? I mean, who cares?

Yeah, I guess.

I don't care, so why do you care?

Yeah. But it's just a fact.

A fact that doesn't matter. Look, I'll put you to sleep, but I'm going to get off on you first. I said in the ad that I wanted a bottom. Do you know what that means?

Yeah, I know what it means.

What does it mean?

Fuck. It means a guy who sucks dick and takes it up the ass.

Then this can't be a huge surprise to you.

No.

Let's face it. If you have a problem being fucked, then you don't really want to die. If you want to die, it shouldn't matter, should it?

No, I guess it's okay. I just . . . forget it.

If it's important to you to die a straight boy in your own mind, fine.

Forget it.

So you want to go ahead and do it?

Yeah. I should, I guess. But look . . .

What?

You said in the ad that if I wanted something . . .

I'm rich if that's what you mean.

You said I should ask.

What can I do for you?

I'd like pay off some debts to some people.

How much do you owe?

Okay, like about $7,000. You don't have to take care of all of that.

No problem.

Seriously?

We'll sit down, figure out all the money you owe, get some money orders, and you can send them off before we do it.

Okay. That's . . . you know, thanks.

But I want some dirty, hot sex for that much money. You agree?

Yeah.

So how soon can we start? Now?

Fuck. Sure.

You scared?

Yeah, I'm fucking scared.

Just come on over.

I should.

Just take a deep breath, and come on over.

Okay. Where do you live?

Evil W top, late 30s, hung and wealthy, into W, H, or A boyish teen bottoms, and looking for the ultimate. Box 157

Dear Box 157, This is a picture of me and my boy. He's 18, I'm 42. If you're really evil, give me a call. I'll explain. Hank 323- *-******

Clark residence.

Can I speak to Hank?

Speaking. Who's this?

The ad guy.

Ad guy?

Box 157.

Hunh.

Hello?

So what are you looking for, . . . what's your name?

The ultimate, like I said.

That's pretty vague.

You're being pretty vague yourself.

Hm.

Hello?

So you liked what you saw in the picture.

What's not to like?

That's nothing.

Yeah?

I'm a twisted son of a bitch.

So that was your boyfriend in the picture?

That's my boyfriend.

Nice.

What?

Your boyfriend.

Oh, yeah.

You said you'd explain.

What's your offer?

My offer? You read my ad. What's your offer?

What do you think?

I don't know. You tell me.

You like my boyfriend.

Yeah.

That's the offer.

Your boyfriend.

Yeah.

You read my ad.

I read your ad. You said you want the ultimate. That's my offer.

Okay. Are we talking about the same thing?

You want to snuff my boyfriend.

Well, yeah.

Then we're talking about the same thing.

Okay. What about you?

Me? I don't want to get snuffed.

No, I mean, what's your deal? What do you get out of it?

Me? Freedom. Money.

I mean, do you want to watch or what?

Hell, yes.

How much do you want?

I don't know. A couple thousand.

Okay. What's his name?

His name? Oh, Antonio. Tony. I call him Fuck.

Does he know about this?

He's my slave.

Okay.

You just have to pull the trigger.

Sounds interesting.

Many have said they would. None have.

Well, I will.

Hold on.

Hello?

Why don't you come by?

You mean now?

Hold on. I'm on the phone, Fuck. You stupid bitch. Hello?

Yeah.

Now's good.

I'm an evil, W, 30s, sadistic, violent, wealthy pedophile type seeking cute young victim. Name your price. Box 157

Box 157, I'll be at the ArcoStation in West Hollywood, corner of Fairfax and Sunset, 2 am, Friday Aug 23. Anonymous

Felix. Wake up. Say hello to Brian.

What?

Here. I'll pull the covers off. Nice, right?

Very nice.

Someone's here to see you. Say hello.

Hello?

Hi.

Get out of bed, Felix.

Okay. Dad?

He looks so young.

It's the pajamas.

Dad, can I lie down?

No, you can't. Take your jammys off.

I was asleep.

Take your jammys off. Felix. I'm not kidding.

Okay.

Not down, off. All the way off.

God, he's adorable.

So you're satisfied.

Yeah, very. But—

Dad?

Just a second, Felix.

He seems sort of . . . I don't know.

Spaced out.

Yeah, he just seems sort of . . . I don't know.

He had an accident. He has a problem.

Dad?

He drowned two years ago. They revived him, but he was dead too long. He used to be a really active kid. Soccer, little league, cub scout, actor. He was in a couple of TV commercials.

Oh, that's it. Right. That's where I saw him.

You saw them.

I just saw one maybe last week.

Jif Peanut Butter.

Yeah, exactly. I knew he looked familiar.

There's a website about him. I don't know if you've seen that. Some pedophile put it together. Actually, I put it up. That's a secret, though. It gets a lot of hits. Mostly fags, but a few girls. They're obsessed with him.

Yeah, I always noticed those commercials.

He got offered a series, a Disney film, a couple of other things. But it was too late.

He can't do it?

No way. Look in his eyes.

Yeah.

Not much there.

They're beautiful eyes.

He looks kind of soulful, doesn't he? Guys say that.

Yeah.

He's not. Or maybe he is, who knows?

He's really something.

So I'm thinking two-five.

Twenty-five thousand?

Yeah.

Dad?

You're joking. That's an insane amount of money.

Look, take as long as you want. Charge your friends to fuck him. Make pornos with him. I don't care.

Dad?

Look, I had to quit my job to be his fucking nurse. He can't eat or take a shit by himself. He can't walk by himself. I'm in debt. I'm totally exhausted.

I'll give you fifteen.

Twenty's the lowest I'm going to go. What, Felix?

Can I sit down?

All right, twenty.

But you have to do it here, tonight.

Here?

Dad?

You can sit down in a minute, Felix.

Fuck that.

And I get to beat the crap out of him first.

Look, I want to take some time on this. He's an amazing kid. There's a lot I want to do.

Then it's twenty- five.

Look . . . Okay, fine.

Good. Felix?

Yeah?

Get dressed.

No, don't. He's great like this.

Dad?

Do what he says, Felix.

Give me your hand.

Okay. Dad?

Later, Felix.

Okay. Bye.

Board

I'd like to begin this message board by proposing we help builtlikeatruck. I'd be willing to forego my next date with an escort and donate the money to help him rebuild his business. If enough of us do the same that could really make a difference. What do you guys say? pppeter

I think pppeter has a great idea. I work in fund raising for a living, and would be willing to coordinate the effort. Let's show the world that the escort loving community is a group of caring individuals, and make a small sacrifice to help out one of our own. diilygob41.

What is this, the Red Cross or something? Give me a fucking break. We're all caught up in this Brad thing because we're obsessed with him and want to fuck him. I want to know where he is and how I can reach him, and so do all of you. Let's get off our high horses and down to business. thetimmonster

I'd be happy to donate part of my escort money to help out builtliketruck, but maybe someone should get in touch with him first and see if he needs or wants our help. Also I want to say to thetimmonster and to everyone else that if we're going to be honest, let's all just admit that we don't want to fuck Brad, we want to kill him. There are hundreds of Brads out there ready to be fucked. We're obsessed with Brad and Brian because the murder thing gives us a boner, and because Brad or Brian or whoever the genius is behind this ridiculous scam knows just how to fuck with our heads. This whole thing is just sick porn and we've all been implicated. Brad's probably a real person, but the Brad we're all obsessed with is a fantasy. Let's admit it and talk openly about our deep dark secret. I'll be happy to start. My secret fantasy is to rape, torture, and kill Nick Carter of the Backstreet Boys. I'd give anything in the world to do that. He's my Brad. Who's yours? boybandluvXXX

Nick Carter, definitely. Wow, I'm not the only one? boybandluvXXX, email me and let's talk about it privately. Nick Carter naked and dead and ice cold in my bed after a night of hot, kinky sex is perfection. For me, early Nick Carter is the ultimate. By early I mean how he looked in that 'Backstreet's Back, All right!' or whatever it's called video. popnfresh

Or even earlier. There are some pictures of Nick at 15 on backstreet.com that practically give me a brain aneurism.

When I imagine Brad, based on the earlier descriptions, I think he must look a lot like early Nick. boybandluvXXX

The freaks come out. Keep it between the sheets, guys. I'm addicted to this saga because it's like a great mystery novel with a lot of sex scenes in it. That's all there is to it. It's like cutting edge escapism. I want to know how it turns out. Who's telling the truth? Who killed Stevie Sexed and why? Why don't some of the actual participants in this whole thing like secretlifer or builtlikeatruck or Renn Adams post here and give us some clues? Am I alone? sammyd

Hi there, fellas. I've been reading this thread, and thought I should post a message here for a couple of reasons. First of all, I appreciate the offer to help me out financially. The truth is that I'm covered by insurance, and, thanks to my loyal and caring customers here in Portland, I'm already in the process of rebuilding my business. The damage was more psychological than financial, but luckily I have some good friends to support me in this tough time. I also thought you'd like to hear an update on the situation with Brad. Like I told you, Brad confessed to the crime, and was in custody awaiting a hearing that would determine the length of his prison sentence. Not long after my last post, Brad's girlfriend Elaine called and asked to meet with me. I did meet with her, mostly hoping to get answers to my questions about why Brad did what he did. After talking to her, I think

I have a much better understanding of the situation. I thought I would share with those of you who are interested. Elaine, who is about fifteen years older than Brad, has known him since he was a kid. She says that he has had serious mental problems since he was very young, and needs seven different prescription medications to remain even relatively stable. She says his mental illness manifests itself in a fixation on older men, and that he has 'gone off the deep end' (her words) and had sexual relationships with gay men since he was eleven years old. She says his pattern has been to become obsessed with gay men, then become violent when they get tired of him. She told me all of this in the hope that I would ask the prosecutor that Brad be given hospitalization rather than prison time. She believes that throwing Brad in with a bunch of criminals and sexual predators would only make Brad's problems worse, as well as endangering his life. Because I think she's right, and because she is pregnant with his child, I did make this request. What I didn't know was that Brad has an extensive arrest record here in Portland for prostitution, assault, stalking, and criminal mischief. Because of his age at the time of the earlier crimes, he was treated leniently, but as he is now sixteen years old (that's official), a prison sentence was 'mandated.' Brad was sentenced (as an adult, shockingly) to eight months in a minimum security prison, but he will receive psychological counseling and will not be housed with the prison's general population unless he misbehaves (whatever that means), at which time his special treatment will be terminated. That's the update. Thanks again for your offer. builtlikeatruck44

Thanks, builtlikeatruck. Can you tell us what prison he's in? Can we write to him? Is he allowed to accept gifts? Can he receive visitors? pppeter

I accessed the Portland Oregonian Newspaper's website (www.portlandoregonian.com) and found out that Brad (last name Gordon) is in Sackamount Prison. I assume you can write to him there and he'll get the letters, as long you don't write anything too nasty. There's even a blurry picture of him. Check it out. zeelyzap

Wow, he may be the cutest boy I've ever seen, at least in that one picture. Does anyone know if the parts in his reviews where he was fist fucked are true? If I could fist fuck the boy in that picture, I would happily die of a heart attack on the spot. builtlikeatruck, if you're still there, does he really look like that? thetempestuoustop

I looked at that picture on the Portland Oregonian site. What are you talking about? You can't even see what he looks like. You're tripping. pppeter

You are a bunch of sickos. Does he look like that? Yeah, he

does. Get your heads out of your crotches for one second. The kid is mentally ill. He's sixteen years old. I don't believe what a bunch of fucking amoral, soulless monsters you are. I'm outta here. builtlikeatruck44

No offense, builtlikeatruck, but we're just fantasizing aloud here. Our fantasy lives are not a police state. We've never met Brad. He didn't burn down our place of business, if I get off imagining my fist in a sixteen year old boy's ass, so what? If I met him, I'd probably feel the way you do, but I haven't met him, and considering the mystery and lies swirling around him, I think he's ripe for any fantasy I want. thetempestuoustop

Fine. Fantasize about anything you want, but don't write him letters and lay your shit on him. That's where it gets amoral. builtlikeatruck44

Hi, everyone. I'm Brad's girlfriend Elaine. I think some of you are mentally ill. I love him, and it scares me to death to know that when he's released from prison, you're going to be out there in the world trying to tempt him into being self-destructive again. Have some compassion, for God's sake. If there are any of you out there who are truly kind and compassionate, Brad has a favor to ask. He's worried about me and our kid, especially now that I'm unemployed. Brad has limited access to email in prison. He's only allowed to correspond with me and his family. He says to tell you that if you are willing to help me out with a donation of $100, you can ask him questions and he will answer them. You would email the questions to me, and I would forward the email to him, and then forward his reply on to you. He will not answer any disgusting sexual questions, just G-rated questions about his day to day life and about his past. If you would be interested in doing this, you can email me at egarrison@hotmail.com for further information. Only serious and decent people please. egarrison

Hey Elaine, before you disappear, is there any chance you'd be willing to answer a few general questions for those of us who can't afford to spare $100, as much we'd like to? I just mean basic things like how he's doing, how you guys met, whether he's straight or bisexual, what you love most about him, and anything you'd be willing to pass along that would help us know the real Brad? Thanks and take care of yourself. knockitoff6

boybandluvXXX and I have started a Kill Nick Carter discussion group. If you're interested in sharing your fatal fantasies about the Rolls Royce of potential corpses, you can join the fun at http://yahoo.com/clubs/nickcarterRIP. popnfresh

I'll make this brief and to the point. I read Elaine's post. I urge you not to trust her. As far as I know, she does not have email access to Brad. No one does. I feel for her situation, and wish her the best, but I think she is scamming you. There are reasons why I think this, but I can't go into them here. builtlikeatruck44

I just wired Elaine $100. Am I screwed? Has anyone else accepted her offer? lonelylarry

Hi guys, this is Elaine. I feel that I have to respond to builtlikeatruck's accusation against me. I am in email contact with Brad, and he will answer your questions. I just sent one of you his answers, so maybe that person can post here and confirm that what I'm doing is legitimate. builtlikeatruck is the liar here. You want to know the truth? I did plead with him to ask the judge in Brad's case for leniency. He refused, and showed no sympathy at all for Brad's medical condition. I was desperate to help Brad, so I did something that I'm not proud of and blackmailed him into helping me. The truth is that he has been deceitful with you from the beginning. He did hire Brad, but not to work at his business. Brad would show up at the work place at noon, and builikeatruck would take Brad back to his house and have sex with him for a few hours, then bring Brad back to the work place where I would pick him up. I didn't like that Brad was returning to that way of life, but we were desperate for money. builtlikeatruck promised Brad he would pay him at the end of the week, and make it seem like he was on the payroll. But the day before Brad was to be paid, builtlikeatruck fired him and refused to pay him for the work he'd done. Not only was this incredibly unfair, but it played right into Brad's mental problems. Brad went to builtlikeatruck's house that night and begged him for the money, and builtlikeatruck finally agreed to pay him in return for sex. Brad went through with it, and builtlikeatruck still refused to pay, and threw Brad out of his house. That's when Brad flipped out and burned down builtikeatruck's business. I told builtlikeatruck I would tell the police that he knowingly had sex with a sixteen year old boy if he didn't help Brad with the judge. That's when he agreed. That's the truth. He's a lying scumbag pedophile, and you shouldn't believe him. egarrison

Here we go again. Could this get any more exciting? mantobeat

I can vouch that Elaine sent me answers to the questions I paid her to ask Brad. Whether Brad answered them himself, I don't know. I will say that in the future Elaine might want to consider cutting and pasting the answers into a new email, because in forwarding me Brad's (or whoever's) email, she inadvertently sent me his address. I won't take advantage of this golden opportunity, but don't think I'm not tempted. I wonder how much I could get for it on eBay? Just kidding, Elaine ;-)) Since I spent my hard earned money on these answers, and you didn't, I'm not going to share them with you. I will say that if Brad wrote the email, he's a very screwed up young man, in a most appealing and sexy way of course. likeemyoung

Alright, Elaine, you asked for it. Elaine is a well known Portland skeezbag who takes in street hustlers, addicts them to heroin, and pimps them to support her and their drug habits. It's true that Elaine has known Brad since he was young, but, as far as I know, they are not now and have never been romantically involved. She is visibly pregnant, but whether the kid is Brad's is anyone's guess. Whether her story about Brad's alleged mental illness is true, I can't tell you, although I do believe that there is a shred of truth in it. The truth is I met Brad when I picked him up in a hustler bar here one night and took him home. I didn't know until much later that he was the Brad everyone had been writing about on this website, since as far as I knew Brad was dead or at least living in Southern California. I also did not know he was under aged until he was arrested, and the truth came out. The sex wasn't fantastic, but I thought he was sweet kid, and gave him a job at my business. Brad was very happy to have found a way out of his hellish life with Elaine. He told Elaine that he was having sex with me everyday, but he was in fact working for me and planned to move out of Elaine's place once he'd earned enough money to get his own apartment. The rest of what happened is exactly as I

explained it to you before. I had sex with Brad only that one initial time, and in no way, shape, or form could it be called S&M. The only thing I didn't mention was that Brad's erratic behavior when he came to my house that night was due in part to the fact that Elaine, who was angry at him for quitting his 'job,' had refused to give him his medication, so he was having withdrawals. I regret not helping him out that night, and I regret lying to you to protect myself, but what's done is done. But if you think she's in contact with Brad, think again. I'm sure your questions are being answered by one or more of her flock of junkie hustlers. Be forewarned.
builtlikeatruck44

Does anyone know the latest on the investigation in Stevie's murder? This whole Brad thing is very amusing, but I'm curious if there's an update on the situation in San Diego.
kellymartin

Well, I couldn't help myself. I wrote an email to Brad at the address that Elaine accidentally forwarded to me, and he wrote back, or somebody did. Is it Brad? See what you think. Here's his email to me: "Dear likeemyoung, It was weird to get an email from somebody I don't know. They said my address was blocked. Elaine is a fuck up, so it's no shock to me that she sent you my address. I'll probably get shit for writing to you but I'm lonely. Thanks for the stuff you said about how I look. I don't get tired of hearing it. I would have killed myself a long time if I didn't look like this. I know about all that shit written about me on that website or most of it. I think it's hilarious. You asked me about Brian. Brian's fucked up, but I love him and I always will probably because he loves me more than anyone else ever did. It's not his fault. I did tell him he could kill me. It was a night when I was really loaded and feeling bad about myself, but I meant it. He started to kill me and I freaked out, but it was my choice not his. It wouldn't make any difference if he had killed me to be honest with you. I'm serious about that. Brian believed in me. He was stupid to believe in me but I'll be honest you, I miss him. I wonder if he knows where I am. It's too late now because Elaine's going to have my kid so I'm going to marry her when I get out of here. You asked if we could hook up for sex when I get out of here, but that depends on how shit goes with her. If she has an abortion then it's for sure. I can give you a call if it doesn't work out. I don't know who builtlikeatruck is. Do you mean Tony the guy I did the arson thing on? I don't know what he's been saying about me. I'm sorry about what I did to him but he kind of played with my head if you know what I mean. He told me he really liked me and it wasn't about sex and I believed him like the stupid fucker I am, but then he turns around and rapes me when I needed a friend. He should be so fucking grateful that I didn't say anything about that to my lawyer. I'm a nice person. I'm just stupid to want people to like me. The good thing about being in prison is no one likes me. There are guys here who want to rape me really bad and let me know about it every fucking minute but they don't say they're in love with me. There's a guy here who wants to kill me and he means it. He's not like all those faggots I used to go with who just wanted to hit me. He's not like all those faggots who wrote all that bullshit about killing me on that website. If some sick, evil motherfucker wanted to kill me and not just talk about it, I'd go for it. I don't mean now because I'm going to have a kid and I want to try to live and love my kid. Fuck it. That's about all I can tell you. Writing to you is making me too depressed. Bye, later. Brad." likeemyoung

Mr. Anthony Villani aka builtlikeatruck (he wishes, btw) has been arrested on charges of child molestation, thanks to me. That's the good news. That bad news is that no thanks to likeemyoung, Brad was caught abusing his emailing privileges and got into a fight with two guards, and has been placed in the general prison population. So not only am I, the mother of his child and his fiancee, unable to talk to him, but his life is in danger. So thanks a whole lot, asshole. So now you freaks can go jerk off thinking about what Brad's probably going through right this very second. I wish all of you a slow, painful death. egarrison

Is this for real? Is that a stupid question?
bobbybebrave

I have an acquaintance who works in the administrative offices of Sackamount prison. I have a call into him. I'll let you know if he can tell me anything about Brad's status. He's gay, so I think he might be willing to share what he knows. snazzystocky

Greetings, everyone. I'm writing an article about Kenneth ('Stevie Sexed') Miller's murder for The Advocate, and thought I'd update you on the latest. I have a source in the law firm Katz and Freiberg, who are representing David ('Corey #3') Barrows in his upcoming murder trial. According to this source, Barrow's attorney will claim that he was hired by Brian Mason Caldwell—aka the 'Brian' of Brad and Brian fame—to assist him in the murder of Kenneth Miller. Barrows' defense team contends that he was addicted to crystal meth at the time of the transaction, and accepted the job only to get money to pay off some drug dealers, but that he never intended to commit the crime. They contend that the murder was committed by Caldwell, and that Barrows was set up to take the fall. But there are several problems with this scenario. The first problem is that the police interviewed Caldwell, and, according to the transcript of this interview, Caldwell contends that Barrows contacted him on numerous occasions in the months prior to Miller's murder offering to sell him a snuff video. He claims that he did eventually agree to buy the video, and arranged to meet Barrows at an apartment in San Diego to complete the sale. He claims that when he arrived, Barrows answered the door in a very disheveled state and covered with what appeared to be blood. According to Caldwell, Barrows confessed that he had never in fact possessed said snuff video, and had in desperation murdered Miller that morning in order to videotape the crime. Caldwell says that Barrows offered to show him Miller's body, which Barrows claimed was somewhere in the apartment, and that he declined and subsequently fled the apartment without buying said videotape. Caldwell also turned over to the police copies of the incriminating emails Barrows had sent him. The second problem is that Barrows's semen was recovered from Miller's bowel and digestive tract, although Barrows' lawyers' contention is that this can be explained as the result of Miller and Barrows having been hired to have sex together by a client on the previous night. They are currently trying to locate the client. The third problem is that the police have been tipped that a videotape of Barrows murdering Miller exists and that copies of this tape are in the possession of several members of San Diego's gay community, although no copies of this tape have turned up thus far. Separate from the investigation, I have been approached by someone who claims to have a copy of this tape and I'm currently in the process of following up on this lead. If anyone out there has any information about the case, they can contact me at zyoung @earthlink.net. thegayjournalist

Oh mama, I would love to see that video. Does that make me an amoral monster? That's a serious question. underthegunguy

It doesn't make you any more amoral than someone who wants to watch a documentary on Nazi concentration camps. As a Jew, I think it's far less amoral. If what we know about Stevie is true, it was possibly consensual and maybe even a mercy killing. The only difference is that Corey or Brian probably weren't feeling merciful at the time. If Stevie really did want to die in a snuff video, as several reports have suggested, wouldn't watching that video be like honoring a dying person's last request? I'd be curious to know if Stevie even fought with his murderer. Who's to say it wasn't the happiest moment of his life? I'd love to see the video too. bergofstrength

I think I saw the video you guys are talking about. It was shown to me at a dinner party last week. Trust me, you don't want to see what I saw. I spent about an hour afterwards vomiting my guts out. I'm into S&M, but this was just nauseating and inhuman. The guy who showed me the tape said the victim was Stevie Sexed, and it did look like him. There were two guys murdering him. Both wore leather hoods, so I can't tell you if one of them was Corey #3. One of them looked about mid-forties and had an eagle tattooed on one of his ass cheeks. The other guy looked about late twenties, and was very well hung. There was at least one other unseen person operating the camera. The victim looked very drugged and not really aware of what was happening. They beat him up and had rough sex until they were all covered with his blood. Then they tied him spread eagle to the bed and the younger guy cut his genitals off while the older guy basically burned his face off with a blowtorch. Then they started caving in his head and chest with metal baseball bats. That's when I couldn't take anymore and threw up and had to leave the room. I feel sick to my stomach even thinking about it, so I'll stop there. justaboy

Eagle tattoo on the ass: Renn Adams, bergofstrength

Or someone trying to make us think he think he's Renn Adams, nottooshabby

Renn Adams makes sense from what we know. Corey, Renn Adams, and Brian behind the camera. ugheustace

Call me sick, but I'd still love to see that tape. underthegunguy

Greetings. Here's an update on what I've learned about the Kenneth Miller murder case. I viewed the videotape that I mentioned to you in my previous post. It would appear to be the same tape described by justaboy. Despite what justaboy said, the victim in this tape is not Kenneth Miller aka Stevie

Sexed. According to the person who showed it to me, the tape has been circulating for about two years. He believes the victim is a San Diego based escort named Kevin who disappeared approximately two years ago. Having studied a rather unclear headshot of Kevin printed in the San Diego Union at the time of his disappearance, I would have to agree. I believe this tape could be the one mentioned by Kenneth Miller in his posts on the old Brad reviews page. I also suspect that one of the men in the tape is in fact Renn Adams. I have a lead on Adams' current whereabouts, and I hope to be able to speak with him in the near future. The other man in the tape does not appear to be Barrows, at least based on my comparison of the man's body to some photographs I have obtained. I continue to believe that a videotape of Kenneth Miller's murder does exist, but its whereabouts are unknown. I would appreciate any credible leads. Also, if Brian Caldwell is reading this, as I suspect he might be, please contact me at the number I left on your phone machine. That's it for now. thegayjournalist

If any of you are interested, I heard from my friend who works at the prison where Brad is serving his sentence. I'll paste his email below.

Dear *******,
There is a 16 year old prisoner here named Brad Gordon. He must be about 5' 9", 120 lbs., dirty blond hair, cute face. I've

heard rumors he whored around on the outside, but a pretty young kid always gets the population excited so I didn't give them much credence. That's quite a story you're spinning there. Another guard here is tight with Gordon, so I ran your questions by him. I was going to tell you that no prisoner here has email privileges, but I guess my coworker has been acting as the middleman between Gordon and some people on the outside. Gordon writes letters then gives them to the guard who types and sends the messages, and when Gordon receives emails the guard prints out hard copies and sneaks them to him. The guard told me he just feels sympathetic for Gordon's tough situation, but a couple of prisoners told me the two are having sex in Gordon's cell at night, and that Gordon is under the guard's protection. They said Gordon has been targeted for a gang rape by about two dozen prisoners, and they're just waiting for the guard to break off the relationship. When I confronted the guard, he admitted he had traded email privileges for sex. I should report this to the warden and get the guard fired, but if I do that, your boy is dead. When kids get gang raped in here, they almost always 'hang themselves.' (The prison reports these deaths as a suicides, and everyone keeps their mouths shut.) The guard offered to set me up with Gordon in return for not reporting him, and I've decided to take him up on it. Before you think I've turned pedophile or something, working here does strange things to your head. When you're around a bunch of ugly, violent, horny men for eight to ten hours a day, a young guy starts to look pretty damned attractive. For me, riding a boy's ass or blowing your load in his mouth can't compete with fucking a man I love, but it's got a charge all its own, I'll give you that much. So I guess that answers your questions. Be a buddy and keep all this between you and me, and I'll give you a taste of what it's like, all right? Henry

How about that shit, huh? Don't worry, I'll share whatever he says with you. You guys owe me, though. snazzystocky

Call me sick if you want but Brad gang raped by a dozen violent criminals then hung by his own belt in a lonely prison cell sounds like the perfect ending to his lying, manipulative, bullshit story to me. I'd give anything to see a video of that. Anyone else agree? vincetheviolet

Fuck that. I want be the one to snuff him. I'm one of the people Brad emails with, and he said I can kill him for $50,000 when he's released from prison. I'm trying to the raise the money. Anyone want to go in with me? killkillkill

Get real, killkillkill. You can't be serious. You're telling us that Brad is selling his life to strangers over the internet with the help of a prison guard? Yeah, I believe that. Take your ridiculous fantasies to that Kill Nick Carter group. We're trying to cut through all the lies swirling around this kid and get to the truth here. pppeter

Fuck you. I'm telling the truth. Here's part of Brad's last email to me if you don't believe me. '. . . I thought about what you wrote, and I've decided you can kill me for $30,000. You'd have to put it in a trust fund for my kid. My girlfriend Elaine is looking into how I can set that up. If you want to videotape it, the price is $50,000. If you're serious about this, I'll put you in touch with her, but don't fucking tell her what the money's for. Just tell her you're a nice rich guy or some shit. I should be out of here in about three months. . . .' Eat shit. pppeter.

Like I said, if anyone wants to go in with me on this, I'm going to need help to raise that kind of money. killkillkill

I agree that this sounds completely implausible, but maybe snazzystocky could ask his prison guard friend to confirm or deny, just so we know for sure? ronaldtrix

I sent my prison guard friend an email asking about this. I'll keep you informed. snazzystocky

How does one write to Brad? I'll gladly pay for the information. On the chance that Brad is reading this, I'll pay you $60,000 if I can snuff you and videotape it. I'm a tax attorney who has experience setting up trust funds, and can help you on that end as well. If you're interested, post a message here, and let me know how to proceed. lawyerguy

Do these two wannabe murderers not realize the police are monitoring this group? Hello?! pppeter

Here's my theory. I think we're right back where we started. Somewhere along the way, this thread of posts was invaded by that Brian character or whoever created 'Brian,' possibly Brad himself, that is assuming Brad is a real person to begin with. We have no proof that the Brad in prison in Oregon is the same Brad who was reviewed on this site, do we? No one ever posted a picture of the original Brad that I'm aware of. We're basing a lot of what we believe to be true on the posts of builtlikeatruck. How do we know he's the real deal? I think the whole story of Brad trading sex for email privileges and this supposed gang of prisoners planning to rape and kill Brad is very far fetched. That sounds like a fantasy of prison life to me. Then there's Brad supposedly agreeing to be murdered for money. Again, it's just so unrealistic. Maybe we should concentrate on the Stevie Sexed murder investigation and drop this whole Brad nonsense, or at least agree that we're playing out a collective fantasy and nothing more. buttons999

I got some reality for you freaks if you want it. I was one of Elaine's friends until last week. The email thing is a scam. Me and two other boys have been writing those guys and saying we're Brad. Elaine hasn't talked to Brad or seen him or anything since he got locked up. The email scam is just for kicks and ripping off the pricks who are fucking stupid enough to believe it. I'm writing this cos Elaine fucked me over good and that bitch can just eat it. I'm also writing cos I got an offer to make to that guy Brian who used to be with Brad if he's reading this (and I know he is). I tried emailing you yesterday but maybe your server's fucked up because you haven't written me back. I have something that you'll very be interested in. I think you know what it is. I want money in return. I think when you see it in person, you'll definitely want it. I'm in Hollywood right now and if you're interested, be at Spotlight bar on Cahuenga at 1 am on this Friday. Just be there and have a beer in your hand and at 1 am put your beer on the jukebox and watch the door. The first guy who walks out the door after that will be me and just leave the bar and follow me on foot at a safe distance and the rest will just happen. Don't try any shit on me and I won't try any shit on you. This is a serious offer. JT

I don't know whether to laugh or cry (LOL). yesman

I don't know whether to moan or groan ;-o. ivantheterrible

This is Elaine. It's very important that all of you read this. It's true that the emailing thing with Brad was a scam. It wasn't my idea, and I regret going along with it. It is over as of right now. A young acquaintance of mine wrote the emails pretending to Brad. His name is Jimmy Taylor and he is the one who posted the message signed JT. Jimmy is a very unbalanced and dangerous boy who works as a prostitute here in Portland. He has a violent temper and has beaten two of his customers in the past, but they didn't report the beatings for the obvious reason. I should have cut off contact with him months ago, but I have a soft heart and thought he was a good kid deep down. Obviously, I made a huge mistake. For the past month, a young neighborhood kid has been hanging around with some of the young street kids who are my friends. Some of the boys befriended him, and he became kind of their mascot. He's a very innocent and naive kid who unfortunately fell lock, stock, and barrel for Jimmy Taylor's egotistical bullshit. He came to really idolize Jimmy, even though Jimmy treated him with nothing but cruelty and contempt. When Jimmy took off, the boy went missing, and Jimmy's post confirms my fear that they are probably together. Another young friend of mine confessed to me this morning that Jimmy has been in email contact with Brad's ex-boyfriend Brian for several months and has been passing along information about Brad. I'm horrified to say that I think Jimmy plans to sell this young neighborhood boy to Brian. I know you guys have some sick fantasies, but this boy is just a sweet and innocent child. Brian, I beg you not to do what he's asking. He may be scamming you, but there's just as good a chance that he is prepared to endanger the boy's life to make some quick money. If you have any decency, you'll call the police or at least take matters into your own hands and do what it takes to get the boy with Jimmy to safety. Think what you want of me, but don't hurt this kid. egarrison

Dear Elaine, The email scam was wrong and selfish of you. You blame your 'young friends,' but you're responsible. That said, I thank God you posted that message and I pray to God that the young boy is safe. Of course by posting that message, chances are that Jimmy Taylor and the boy are long gone. Just in case, four friends of mine and I will be at the Spotlight bar on Friday, prepared to do whatever it takes to capture Jimmy Taylor and turn him into the police. Be assured that my friends and I will do everything we can. Could you post descriptions of the two boys? It's possible that I or someone else in the Hollywood area could spot the pair and alert the police. Thanks, and pray for us all. goodandplenty

I thought you'd like to know that Jimmy Taylor is not a problem anymore. I took care of it. I sent in a review if you want to know the details. Check under Jimmy #2 in the Portland section. It's the newest (fifth) review, dated yesterday. The boy with Jimmy is safe for now. Well, he's alive anyway. I need to get some sleep because I'm exhausted. If you read the review, you'll understand why. Later, guys. someoneone

I read the Jimmy 'review.' That is some sick, sick shit. Brian, is that you? It has your earmarks. hotgiant

Look at this way: at least Jimmy finally got a positive review. Sweet dreams. someoneone

I'm one of the suckers who wasted good money on Jimmy #2 from Portland. See my review, dated last April 18th. If someoneone did what he says, then he'll be able to describe a very unusual tattoo that Jimmy has (or had?) and where it is (or was?) located on his body. pozandproud

I just want to let you know that our Kill Nick Carter group is really cooking and you guys ought to check it out and join in on the fun. If Nick isn't your thing, how about his stunning little bro Aaron Carter? He's fair game too. Want to know what happens when a naked, drugged Nick is thrown into a lion's cage? Maybe you prefer the story of the psycho surgeon who finds a naked, anesthetized Aaron on his operating table? Sound good? You know it does. boybandluvXXX

Okay, someoneone, put it out there or get your mind games out of here. masteringmike

Since chances are you're lying through your teeth, whoever you are, I'm embarrassed to say this, but you shouldn't do to that boy what you did to Jimmy Taylor. Why, you ask? Because you've killed enough for one night, and I dare you to convince yourself and us why you should kill him. The reasons not to do it are obvious. I'd like hear you justify such an evil act. Maybe you think you can justify Jimmy Taylor's murder by arguing that he brought it on himself but how do you justify killing an impressionable, innocent boy who did you no harm? marcfromphilly

This guy sounds like he's killed before. I'd like him to tell us who he is. He probably just wants attention. Talk to us and let the boy go. pppeter

His story is a bunch of crap. Prove it, you liar. snazzystocky

Just so you all know, my friends and I went to Spotlight tonight, and did what Jimmy Taylor asked, and nothing happened. I don't know what it means, but Jimmy Taylor either didn't show or chickened out. I just got home, and brought a hustler back with me, so this will be quick, but that's what the story is on my end. goodandplenty

I just had a nice, long sleep and feel a whole lot better. I have to go get my broken fingers (see review) looked at, but I thought I'd say hi. Prove it? James Taylor. Hair: blond, eyes: blue. I didn't measure him, but he was about 5' 9", maybe 130 lbs. He had the word Tool tattooed in his right armpit, and a big, ugly scar on his left ankle. The other kid says his name is Phillip Berringer and that he's 13 years old. He seems to be a hippie or the son of hippies, and was wearing a tie-dyed t-shirt, baggy old jeans, and leather sandals when he arrived. He has long, straight brown hair, green eyes, a cute elfin, turned up nose and this really pretty little ass. He's vegan and claims he has been since birth. I'm guessing that explains why his ass has such a sweet, delicious aroma. I'm no scat queen, but I'm definitely going to sample what's up that hot little ass. What else do you need to know? He's still alive, obviously, and I'm waiting to be convinced why he should remain so. Don't wait too long. someoneone

Call me crazy, but I also think this is Brian of 'Brian and Brad.' There's just something about his posts that starts bells ringing in my head. Are you the Brian of Brad and Brian? Fess up. xtacyla

Again, I ask you to justify your actions. You can't, can you? marcfromphilly

As the person who asked this psycho to prove he killed Jimmy Taylor, I should tell you that his 'proof' consists of information that is readily available in Jimmy #2's reviews. Even the tattoo in the armpit is described there. I just hadn't noticed it before. Again, I say this guy is full of shit. pozandproud

I'm a friend of Elaine and she asked me to write because she's too upset. She wants to say the guy who says he killed Jimmy Taylor knows too much about him and it must be true. I want to say to the guy please don't hurt Philly if you really have him. We call him Philly but his name is Phillip Berringer. We really care about him and he's not a hustler or anything like that but just a sweet little person. We put all our money together and we have almost $5000 we can pay the guy if he lets Philly go. The guy can email me at xtracutebill@aol.com or write a message to me here. If he wants something else instead he can just ask. xtracutebill

Dear xtracutebill, We can negotiate for Phillip, but no emailing. I'm not an idiot. Also, just so you know, money's not what I want. Be online between 9 and 11 pm tonight and I'll send you an instant message. We'll chat and see what we can figure out. Now excuse me. I have a 13 year old virgin to fuck. someoneone

Wait, so this is real? I've just been thinking it was a bunch of bull. What do we do now, call the police? pppeter

I still say it's a bunch of bull. I've never killed anyone, obviously, but that guy's review of Jimmy Taylor is pure porn. It was obviously written by someone who was fantasizing about doing those things, not someone who'd just killed a boy and dismembered him, and who supposedly is completely exhausted and has three broken fingers. It doesn't make sense that he'd still be so hot and bothered about a boy after he'd dismembered him. He'd feel guilty or regretful or disgusted or indifferent even, but not hot to trot about how cute he was. It's not logical at all. It's a cruel mind game. snazzystocky

I've never posted before and I won't post again, but I killed a boy once, and I can tell you that I still masturbate thinking about him four years later. That guy's post rang true to me. Unless you've killed a boy, you have no idea how hot it is, and how the boy you killed becomes the ultimate sex object forever. Maybe it doesn't make sense, but it happens. It takes all my willpower not to kill another boy. I believe him and, as sick as it may sound to you, I envy him. God give me strength. nobodyatall

To the change the subject slightly, so what's the real story on Brad? Does anyone know? Is he still in prison? jimgimz

To someoneone, I've thought about your offer, and I think we can work something out. I'll be online from 7 pm until you IM me. xtracutebill

xtracutebill, Can you let us in on this? You probably can't, right? I'm sure a lot of us are anxious to know. goodandplenty

If the anonymous poster really is Brian, which I don't believe, what happened to him? He used to play himself as a nice, emotional guy who had sick sexual fantasies. Now he just sounds like a cold hearted psychopath. That's the main reason I don't think he's the same person. Explain. simperingsam

someoneone, the answer is yes. Tell me how do this. I'll be online until midnight. xtracutebill

Hey builtlikeatruck, can anyone visit Brad? easygoer

To answer xtacyla's question, yeah, I'm Brian. You want to know why I changed? Because Brad broke my fucking heart. Brad crushed my soul and twisted my mind. I loved that beautiful, selfish, lying, manipulative, psychotic young prick. If there's any feeling left in me, I still love him. I kill boys because I hate them for not being him. The hatred I feel when I rape and humiliate and torture and beat and dismember their beautiful young faces and bodies is as close as I can get to the fury of love I felt for Brad. The thing about Brad is that he was right—killing a boy who wants to die is an experience beyond any other in the world. I've had some of the most sexually intense, profound experiences that anyone has ever had, and I know the ugly truth of what life really means. Brad convinced me that he wanted me to kill him because it would mean he and I were both truly loved, and that I haven't achieved, and that's the only thing will stop me because I know that is what I need. I shouldn't say it's the only thing that will stop me because I now believe that he was lying to me, and that it will be nearly impossible to find that perfect love. What will stop me is killing Brad. I'm going to kill him. There's nothing you or he or anyone he knows can do about it. I'm going to do whatever it takes to find him and snuff out his exquisite and sadistic life, and in the meantime I'm going to get my rocks off by continuing my quest for the penultimate murder. If Brad has any humanity in him, he will give himself to me to save the lives of all the boys who are going to die until he's dead. Because I'm a highly intelligent, resourceful, and very wealthy guy, and the police will not be able to stop me. Writing this will not lead the police to me. I've made sure of that, but go ahead and following my 'leads' if you want. So there you go, you losers. Oh, if it matters to you, Phillip Berringer is still alive and intact, but he is not the boy he used to be. I've spent most of the last 24 hours pounding his little ass with my thick 9 1/2" cock. I've buried most of my hand in his hot, cramped hips, and heard his anal muscle tear apart, and seen his bloody asshole gnaw toothlessly at my knuckles. He is running a high fever, and is very pale and sweaty and weak, but it just makes him look more beautiful. He doesn't fight me very much anymore, and I think he even enjoys the sex. If the deal with xtracutebill falls apart, I think I'm going to enjoy every endless second of killing him. Does anybody out there have any suggestions? Hopefully, it won't come to that. someoneone

Message to Brian: Greetings. This is thegayjournalist. I've

been trying to contact you for an interview. You haven't responded to my messages, but you seem to be very open about discussing your crimes and fantasies in this forum, so I thought I'd try asking you a few questions, and you can respond to them here if you'd prefer. I would appreciate it. Here are my questions, (1) Were you involved in the murder of Stevie Sexed. If so, can you tell me how you did this and why, and explain what part if any David (Corey #3) Barrows played in the murder? (2) Was the murder videotaped? (3) What part if any did Renn Adams play in the murder of Stevie Sexed? (4) Were you involved in the murder of the escort known as Kevin? (5) Is there nothing I can do to persuade you to meet with me? If you want, you can send me an instant message any evening this week except Wednesday between the hours of 7 pm and 3 am. My AOL screen name is balticsea7. Thank you for your consideration. thegayjournalist

To xtracutebill, Acknowledgement. Let's do this. As agreed, but change 7 to 9, 1134 to 873, remove 'stan.' 20 minutes. brian

P.S. to Brian (and everyone else): I wasn't going to mention this, but on second thought, why not? I have a wild (?) theory that I want to run by Brian and all of you who might be interested in responding. Even though I can't substantiate this theory in this forum, my gut tells me that Stevie Sexed and Brian's Brad are the same person. In other words, Brad is dead and the Brad in Portland that you're all obsessing about isn't the same guy. I think Brad/Stevie was killed by that reviewer who claimed to have killed him in the old thread of Brad reviews. I think the suspicion around Corey is a red herring. I think Corey probably killed the escort Kevin (and probably others) and is lying about the Stevie Sexed murder in order to get immunity for the Kevin murder. I think whoever killed Brad/Stevie falsified the latter reviews and postings about Stevie in the Brad review thread to draw attention away from his deed. I think Renn Adams was involved, just as the reviewer claimed. Why else would he flee the United States, as it appears he has done? I don't think Brian was involved in Brad/Stevie's murder. I think Brian honestly believes that Brad is still alive. I say all of this to tell Brian that he should meet with me and tell me his side of the story as a way to clear up the suspicion around him. thegayjournalist

Elaine, I'm here. Call my cell phone ASAP. xtracutebill

Elaine, Since you're a junkie, and Bill's a decent bottom, I'll give you the benefit of the doubt, but if you don't call his cell phone to confirm within the next two hours, the deal's off, and he and Phillip are sentenced to death. brian

Elaine, YOU FUCKING CUNT, HE'S GOING TO KILL ME IF YOU DON'T CALL ME IN 30 MINUTES!!!! CALL ME, CALL ME, CALL ME!!!!! PLEASE!!!! xtracutebill

Elaine, You are a very, very stupid woman. Do you think this little game of silence will save Brad? I know he was released early from prison, bitch. Avoiding me won't help him, and you're sacrificing human lives for nothing. I don't need your help anyway. Your whore Bill has helped me. You were willing to sacrifice him, and he's very happy to sacrifice Brad to earn more money as my informant than he could have ever earned working as your whore. Thanks to him, I'm tracking Brad's location as we speak. I know how to contact him, and I'm just waiting for the right moment. I expect to be back in contact with him within days or weeks. If you think he'll choose you over me and what I have to offer, then you're very foolish. As for Phillip, he'll be dead by the morning. I want to kill that cute little hippie bitch more than you've ever wanted to do anything in your life, so thank you for the thrill. And to thegayjournalist, I'll try to answer your questions tomorrow. brian

I still don't buy it. Anybody else agree? pppeter

I know the webmaster of this site doesn't want to get involved in all of this, but I miss his reality checks. Can or will he help us out at all? anaccountant

Okay, this is interesting. Check out The Oregonian newspaper online (www.oregonian.com). In the local news archive, there's an little item that says one Brad Gordon, 16, was released from Sackamount Prison three weeks ago now. It says that the unnamed person against whom Brad committed the crime for which he was imprisoned lobbied for his early release. Doesn't this seem to confirm Brian's last post? ohbarry

Obituary: Phillip Lawrence Berringer, 13, died at 7:22 am this morning after a long battle with his kidnapper. The official cause of death is unknown, although witness accounts suggest he died of massive internal injuries. At the time of his death, he was blind, deaf, and paralyzed from the neck down due to a severe spinal cord injury suffered on the previous night. Berringer was a cute brunette boy of average intelligence who never amounted to anything. brian.

P.S. Oh, I almost forgot to answer thegayjournalist's questions. Was I involved in the death of Stevie Sexed? Here's a sketch for you. Early on in the so-called 'Brad saga,' Stevie (I forget his real name, and who gives a fuck?) started spamming me with emails wherein he offered himself as 'the ultimate bottom' for a rather large sum of money. As I've explained, I'm loaded and don't mind paying for what I want, but I'm not stupid. We exchanged a few emails. He clarified that I could 'snuff' him for a price, but he refused to explain why money had to be involved, since he would be dead and beyond material things. His other stipulation was that the murder had to be videotaped for posterity. I was intrigued, but I was involved with Brad at the time and only interested in killing him, so I stopped responding to Stevie's emails after a while. Around that time, he started posting on Brad's reviews thread, and 'reviews' of him started appearing there as well. It was quite clear to me that this was a game he was playing to get me to take him up on his offer. In retrospect, I'm convinced that Stevie was responsible for most of the erroneous reviews and posts that made the thread of Brad reviews go so haywire. Then Brad betrayed me and disappeared, and, of course, Stevie immediately started writing me again offering to be snuffed. By then Stevie's advanced AIDS and its effect on his mind and body were apparent to everyone, so I was wary that he wasn't the cute little porn star anymore. But I was extremely angry and depressed over losing Brad, and saw Stevie as one of the causes for this loss. I should also say that during this time I had become friendly with Renn Adams, and he had confessed his participation in two snuff videos. It seems the reviewer who mentioned the snuff videos was an ex of Renn's who was using those false reviews to get back at Renn. For me, Renn was a great person to talk to since he'd actually killed two boys and could coach me on what to expect when I eventually murdered Brad, and because he'd done that SM scene with Brad, so we could compare notes. A couple of days after Brad disappeared, Renn called me and said he was fleeing the country due to paranoia that the publicizing of his involvement in the snuff industry on this site would lead to his arrest. He came by for a last visit, and gave me some of his SM toys as well as his copies of the two snuff videos. I was weighing Stevie's offer at the time, and Renn suggested that if I decided to snuff Stevie, I should get in contact with a friend of his, the escort Corey #3, who had recently posted on this site about doing a threesome with Stevie. Renn said Corey was very interested in getting involved in the snuff industry. I phoned Corey, and he agreed to arrange a situation where we could snuff Stevie in return for a sum of money. Part of this plan involved Corey posting a series of erroneous reports on this site about Stevie's supposed possession of a snuff video, and Corey's intention to watch this video, and his finding a mysterious man in Stevie's apartment who'd claimed he'd murdered Stevie. The problem was that Corey is a fucking idiot who began implicating me as a way to protect his own ass, apparently not realizing that he was implicating himself as well, since we had been emailing about our plan. If any of you are serious computer wizzes, you might know how simple it is to alter documents, including emails, in such a way that the alteration is undetectable. So I went back and altered our correspondence to set Corey up for the fall. I had been covering my own tracks from the very beginning. Anyway, Corey told Stevie there was a john who would pay big money to do an SM scene with both of them, with the John and Corey playing the masters and Stevie playing the slave. Of course Stevie was more than agreeable. Renn had put me in touch with a man who had a dungeon which he rented out for private snuff scenes and snuff video shoots, and I'd arranged to rent it for 24 hours. Corey picked up Stevie and drove to a prearranged location where I met them. Then I blindfolded both of them and drove all three of us to the location of the dungeon. Corey was angry about being kept in the dark about the location, but I explained that this was a prerequisite of the owner, and he did eventually agree to this precaution. Let me say that Stevie's AIDS and heavy drug use and willingness to let johns beat the shit out of him had taken a toll on his looks, but he was still quite cute in a kind of disturbing way, if you don't mind them very thin. But he was way too chatty and hyper for my taste, and I had to stop the car and punch him in the head a couple of times to shut him up. When we got to the location, the guy who owned the dungeon took the blindfolded boys and me inside and I paid him. I forgot to mention that for an extra fee, the dungeon's owner will videotape the snuff scene, and I'd arranged for that as well. So before Stevie's blindfold came off, Corey and I put on these latex hoods, and the guy started filming. Corey and I walked Stevie to the center of the room and manacled his wrists to these chains hanging from the ceiling, then took his shoes and socks off, and chained his ankles to the floor, and removed his blindfold. When he saw the room and our hoods and the videotaping, he kind of freaked out. I guess it was pretty obvious he wasn't going to get out of there alive. He didn't beg us to let him go or anything, but he started crying and hyperventilating, and at the same time it was like he was trying to control himself and calm down. I was just kind of amazed by the gravity of the whole thing, since it was all new to me. But Corey got all macho and started telling Stevie he was a pathetic AIDS whore and he deserved to die, and that no one cared, and that no one would remember him and so on. Weirdly, that seemed to calm Stevie down and he started smiling and even laughed a couple of times at some of Corey's crueler remarks. I thought the whole thing was just great and beautiful, and even the guy who owned the dungeon seemed impressed. He kept saying the equivalent of wow and filming Stevie like he was some fashion model or something. There was a point when it seemed like it was all good with everyone, including Stevie, and then we started it and there was no turning back. In retrospect I think the whole thing was rather crude and full of wasted opportunities, but its power was undeniable, especially when I watched the videotape, because the guy did a great job of filming it. It was very SM in style of course, because of where it took place, which was interesting and hot, though I've come to prefer a much freer and more personal style of murder because it really brings home that you're killing an individual. Anyway, Corey and I just basically huddled around Stevie doling out violence with whips and stun guns and metal bats. There was so much blood after a while that I had to step back because I didn't want that piece of shit whore to give me AIDS. Corey, who I assume was already infected, didn't give a shit. At one point he sliced off Stevie's balls and accidentally cut his hand in the process, but he didn't care, and there was blood splattering all over him and even into his mouth. I was sort of amazed by how long Stevie lived. He was conscious, although completely out of it, right up to the end. After about ninety minutes of this, Stevie was so mentally gone and ugly that I just said, It's over, let's do it. I took Stevie's back and Corey took Stevie's front, and we just plunged knives into him until his dead body was hanging limp in the chains. I'd brought a body bag with me, and Corey zipped Stevie's corpse inside it, and we carried it out to the car and put it in the trunk. The dungeon guy let Corey and I shower, then we drove to Stevie's apartment and posed his body on his bed and left. I drove Corey back to his car, paid him, and that was that. So there's your answer. Let me add that I never told Stevie that I was Brian, and I kind of regret that. I would love to have seen his reaction. Also, I have no idea who this Kevin person is, and I definitely didn't kill him. It's possible that Corey might have killed him, because Corey told me that he was paid by someone to kill a fellow escort. If so, it wasn't a sex killing, as I understand it, but more of a hit. Lastly, what would be the point of meeting with you, thegayjournalist? It seems like a huge risk on my part with no reward whatsoever. That's all I have to say for now. brian

Brian, I think you're full of crap. If you had killed Stevie Sexed somewhere else and put his body in his apartment, you think the police wouldn't know that? Haven't you ever watched those forensics shows on TV? Your whole bullshit story stinks. It's a brilliant con job, but it's just a little too imperfect around the edges. Nice try. digereedoodon

Hey idiot, do you really think the police tell the public everything they know? Get a life. brian

Greetings, everyone. Based on information I've received from a source in the San Diego Police Department, the police have long known that Kenneth Miller was not murdered where his body was found, although this information has not been made public. Even more interestingly, this same source tells me that there is a plea bargain already in the works whereby David Barrows will plead guilty to second degree murder in the contract killing of escort Kevin King and agree to testify against Brian Caldwell in the Kenneth Miller murder case in return for a lenient prison sentence. An arrest warrant has been issued for Brian Caldwell, and a manhunt is under way. So is my "wild" theory about Brad/Stevie starting to ring a little more true? Now to speak to Brian directly: You should meet with me because I'm an interesting, intelligent, nonjudgmental person that I think you would enjoy talking to. If it helps, people say I'm very attractive. I'm 22 (but look younger), 5′ 10″,

155 lbs., blond hair, blue eyes. You can see some pictures of me on my homepage: http://hometown.aol.userpage/zackyoung. Maybe most importantly, I happen to have survived an assault and attempted murder by a well known serial killer when I was fifteen, and I think you might be interested to hear the perspective of a someone who's been in that position. So there are some reasons to meet with me. You have my contact information. thegayjournalist

Allright, thegayjournalist, you and your pictures in particular have persuaded me. Be online tonight between 7 pm and 10 pm and I'll instant message you, and we'll see what we can work out. brian

Greetings you sick motherfuckers, this is Jimmy Taylor. You heard me right. I'm in an internet cafe in Tucson. I was gonna let you faggots stew in your sick juices, but it's just too fucking hilarious. I'm really just writing this to let Elaine know we're okay. Nobody killed me. I've just been driving around the southwest here having a fucking good old time. Somebody's screwing with you. That Brian guy never hooked up with me. I never even heard from him. I wasn't gonna let him kill anybody. If you want to know the honest to God fucking truth, I was gonna rob the motherfucker. All I know about him is what Brad told Elaine. I don't even know if the fucker is for real. There's no Bill or xtracutebill who worked for Elaine either. Nobody worked for Elaine anyway. She's just a nice lady who's into helping fucked up young guys. That's all bullshit. She had second thoughts about my emailing with Brad scam and so I took off with the money we'd earned. That's all there is to it. If any of you freaks live in Tucson and want to hook up with me, my pager is 520-526-8221. I'm versatile, hung 8", 19 years old, cute, and a great top or bottom. $150 hr./$500 overnight. Page me. jimmytaylor

I have a theory and I'm just going to throw it out there because I think it offers a decent explanation. Let's say theoretically that there is a Brian, although that's certainly not his real name. He has been posting messages under various guises using a number of different email accounts and screen names. Let's break it down: the main contributors to this thread have been Brian, builtlikeatruck, Elaine, thegayjournalist, snazzystocky, xtracutebill (who we now know is probably not real). Am I forgetting someone? What if these 'people' and one or more of the minor posters are really one person? It's entirely possible, don't you think? It would explain why there's been nothing, zero, in the media about all the missing persons and murders and murder investigations that have been presented here as real events. I'm a media junkie, and I've been looking in vain for a single of mention anywhere in the print, broadcast, or online media of the supposed murder investigation that thegayjournalist claims is going on. Do you really think in this day and age of sensational news that this would escape the media? In fact, the last mention I was able to find of Stevie's murder was shortly after his death, and it was tiny piece in the Los Angeles Times claiming the police no leads whatsoever. That's just one example. I've lived in Eugene, Oregon for twenty-five years and am very familiar with Portland's escort and street hustler scene, and no one I know in that scene has ever heard of this Elaine character or any of these boys except for Jimmy Taylor. It's a small community, and there's no way that she or her boys could exist without anyone in the scene knowing about it. Not to mention the fact that the whole set up of the motherly junkie pimp and her boys just sounds like some pervy Dickens fantasy. Are you getting the picture? This whole thing is a dupe, possibly even perpetrated by the person or persons who run this site. There is only one curious truth in all of this, namely that there is in fact a 16 year old named Brad Gordon who was convicted of the crime of arson. He was released from Sackamount Prison a month ago. I admit that that this fact does raise very interesting questions, and suggests that there might well be someone out there who is obsessed with Brad Gordon and using this site as a forum to spin fantasies about him, but that's all it suggests. thestinge

Wow, that makes so much sense. Thanks, thestinge. pppeter

I feel like a fool (LOL). popnfresh

Hey Brian, let's hear you counter that one, you freak. nastyned

Hey guys, I'm real, and my posts have been real and truthful. thestinge has a point, but if there is a scam, I'm not part of it. builtlikeatruck44

In the spirit of getting to the bottom of this, I have a confession. I made the whole thing up about having a relative who works in the prison. I was just having some fun, but I apologize for the confusion. I did write to 'Brad,' and 'Brad' did write back to me as I said, although I guess it was probably that Jimmy Taylor character who wrote the email I shared with you. But I am a real person. snazzystocky

Message from the Webmaster: I have decided to eliminate this discussion group. This site was established to provide a service to the community, but it is also a business. The fact is that I receive far more emails complaining about this particular message board than emails showing support for it. I allowed you to set up this board because, despite the complaints I received about the thread of Brad reviews, there was tremendous interest in the Brad and Brian 'saga,' and the traffic on this site was greatly increased due to that interest. This is no longer the case, and in fact this discussion group is now creating an attrition in the traffic to this site as well as an unwieldy amount of hate mail directed at me personally. I can't speak to the veracity of any of these posts, but on the chance that there is some truth here, I think ending this board will be in the best interest of everyone who posts reviews or messages here. Let's face it: prostitution is illegal. The authorities tend to look the other way when prostitution goes on in a private manner, and this site has not been directly threatened with closure yet. I have received no contact from the authorities since I removed the thread of Brad reviews, which might tell you something in and of itself. But for me to allow this group to continue risks drawing unwanted attention, and it's simply not a gamble I'm willing to take any longer. There are plenty of places on the internet where you can establish a group to continue this discussion, and I suggest you do so. I'll give you until midnight tomorrow to say your goodbyes and make plans to continue this discussion elsewhere, and then this entire thread will be removed from the site.

Oh damn. (Calm down, girl.) Listen, you nasty, evil fellas are more than welcome to join the Kill Nick Carter group (www.yahoo.com/groups/nickcarterRIP) and keep the debate going there. To be honest with you, the group has sort of run its course and we could some fresh input. There are only twelve members, and we've run out of entertaining snuff fantasies. Still, I have to admit that I'd love to hear how Brian would snuff our Nick (or his little bro Aaron Carter) if he feels like sharing. Hope to see you all there. boybandluvXXX

Okay, but are there any other options? Anyone want to start a group or club just for us? snazzystocky

You guys crack me up. Note to Nick Carter queen: Listen, babe, if I kill your boy, it'll be for real. Don't go planting ideas in my head. I'd love a real challenge at this point. Don't tempt me. brian

Oh, please. boybandluvXXX

Go for it, Brian. Do it for the real music lovers of the world. I dare you. triflewithtom

What, are you nuts, triflewithtom? What if Brian is the real deal? Don't play with fire. It's not funny. boybandluvXXX

Guys, I highly recommend you check out thegayjournalist's homepage. He is a total babe. Hubba hubba. oscarsorifice

No kidding. Hey, thegayjournalist, if you ever need a little extra cash, email me at pinchme37@juno.com. pinchme37

I've never posted here before, but the earlier post from thestinge inspired me to throw in my two cents. Consider this a clarification of one or two points in thestinge's reality check. I live in Portland and happen to be friends with a woman named Elaine. She is a thirty-eight year old massage therapist who is engaged to marry a much younger man named Brad Gordon. Until about a month ago, Brad was serving a sentence at Sackamount Prison. He is now free and living with Elaine, who is pregnant with his child. Until about a year ago, Elaine worked as a counselor to local street kids, and Brad was one of her clients. She says Brad was living off and on at that time with a gay man here in Portland, and that when the man got a new job in Los Angeles, Brad relocated with him. She hadn't heard from Brad in about eight months when he showed up in Portland this last September. Soon thereafter, she became pregnant by him, and they decided to get married. Elaine told me that when Brad was living in Los Angeles, he went off his medication, and wound up working as prostitute. Now, clearly these facts have appeared in this thread of posts, although in a very distorted form. If you'd ever met Elaine, you would laugh at the idea that she could ever be accused of pimping or using hard drugs. She's just a good hearted, eccentric woman who has opened her heart and home to a bunch of street kids who have nowhere else to go. In my opinion, they've done nothing but take advantage of her generous and loving nature. Unfortunately, in the case of Brad, I feel she has been taken in by a very manipulative, charismatic, and dangerous young man. I've met Brad on a number of occasions, and while he is physically attractive, I don't buy his little lost boy act for a moment. He is an A1 sociopath and user who literally reeks of creepiness and generally bad vibes. I personally think he must be behind all of this. I don't know else how to explain the fact that whoever is perpetrating this scam knows so much about his current life. By the way, I am a real person, if you want proof, feel free to visit my homepage at http://aol.com/homepages/earljackson. earljackson

See you all in the Nick Carter group? mumblymerrick

I looked at the gay journalist's website the other day thinking to myself that one of the pictures looked really familiar. This morning I was surfing some gay websites and I came across a personal ad for a guy named 'Zack Young' in West Hollywood. Bingo. Same picture. See for yourself. His ad is listed on 911formen.com. Click 'Classifieds,' then click 'Rough Date,' then click 'California,' then click 'West Hollywood.' Interesting. piercingscream

Since this board has only a couple of hours to live, let's say that unless someone posts a better option, we all join the Nick Carter group, okay? Pathetic, I know. Is it a deal? puffnfresh

Before you guys think about hooking up with Zack Young, you should know he has an eyebrow raising profile on the sites bareback.com, barebackcity.com, and barebacksex.com. And I quote: Gorgeous poz top seeks cute, slender, 18-20 year old neg bottoms for breeding. I'll pound your throat and ass raw with my fat 11" cock then shoot huge loads of poz cum in your ravaged holes. Sero-conversion guaranteed. Also seek serious relationship with a cute, 18-20 year old poz bottom into pneumonia scenes, death dance, lesion wearing, and grave chase. I pay for room, board, medical bills, . . . funeral? Have you heard enough? donutsfordan

Hi everybody, READ THIS, THIS IS IMPORTANT. I'm a former fuck buddy of the 'Zack Young' you guys are talking about. (BTW, DO NOT GET INTO A REGULAR THING WITH ZACK. He's gorgeous and the best top I've ever tricked with in my life, but the less well you know him personally the better, believe me! Don't make my mistake!!) Now, I don't know this for absolutely certain, but I'm 99% sure that Zack has been posting here under the guise of a journalist. In the months that I dated Zack, he was obsessed with the discussion on this particular message board. I started reading it every now and then it to see what he was talking about, but I didn't put two and two together until this morning when I caught up on the last dozen or so posts. Zack is a diagnosed obsessive compulsive. His current fixation is the Stevie Sexed murder, including the whole 'Brad' and 'Brian' nonsense. Ever since I met 'Zack,' he maintained that he was almost murdered by a serial killer when he was in his teens. Whether this is true or not, I don't know. But I do know this: HE IS NOT A JOURNALIST. I know this delusion of his quite well, but I had no idea that he might be acting out his delusion on this message board. He is a rather brilliant man with an extremely high IQ. Until he was fired from his job six months ago, he was a high level software designer at IBM. People have suggested that someone might be masterminding this thread, and I can only say that 'Zack' possesses the computer skills to do something like that. Honestly, I think he lacks the mental organization to pull something like this off, but it is technically possible. I just thought you should know. hotbarehole4you.

So what was real? pppeter

I've been reading this message board with fascination and even a kind of pride at what I've inspired. I thought the lies and fabrications posted in the old Brad reviews were crazy, but this is beyond the beyond. Call me a spoil sport, but I have to give you all some bad or maybe good news. This is Brian. The real, original, true Brian. I have never posted on this message board. None of the things 'I've' supposedly written here are true. My last real and honest post about Brad was my final statement in the now defunct Brad reviews. I'm not under suspicion for the murder of Stevie Sexed, as far as I know. I certainly didn't kill him. I don't know any more about this Corey person than you do. I didn't meet with Jimmy Taylor. I thought about going to the bar that night just to get a look at him, but I didn't. I did call his pager a few days ago to see if he knew how I could get in touch with Brad, and he helped me out for a small sum. Here is all the truth I know about Brad since we broke up. I have not been in touch with him directly as of yet, but a friend of mine in Portland ran into him recently and discovered the following: Brad was convicted of arson, spent some months in prison, and is now free and married to a woman named Elaine who's pregnant, seemingly with his child. The rest of what has been claimed here is undoubtedly fabricated or wildly distorted. The person who is impersonating me (and others, I would imagine) has quite the imagination. You would never understand what I've been through. It's nothing like the ludicrous, emotionless snuff pornography you've been reading here. You're all lost in your own imaginations. I was lost in my imagination for a long time too. I'm trying to get away from that now. I'm not sure that I will ever see Brad again or want to see him. I think about writing to him just to see how he's doing, but I haven't. That's all you will ever know about Brad's and my long lost relationship. Believe me or don't believe me. I could care less, to be honest with you. If the journalist who keeps posting here wants to contact me and hear the real story, he can email me. I'd be happy to answer any questions he has. therealbrian

Greetings, everyone. Okay, you win. I've been hoaxing you. I'm not writing an article for The Advocate. I don't know any more about the Stevie Sexed murder than any joe who reads the newspaper. I made most of that up, although I do think my theory is a good one. I'm just obsessed with the whole Brad/Brian/Stevie Sexed mythology like you guys. The difference is that I won't sit on the sidelines with my tongue hanging out. Yep, I've been posting here in the guise of Brian and a number of other key players. I'll let you guys figure that out. It's been fun making you pant and squirm and scratch your heads. But I got what I came for. (The real?) Brian has given me a way to contact (the real?) Brad in Portland and I should know pretty soon what's true, not to mention hopefully getting myself a piece of that infamous ass. Brian also kindly answered some key questions about their relationship that will help me out a lot in my dealings with Brad. The profile I posted on those bareback sites is a year old, and I've moved on to other things. Still, if there's a pretty young thing out there who wants to be bred, drop me a line and photo and I'll consider it. Here's some good news for you. If everything goes as planned, Brad may be back in business and rentable soon. You're welcome, guys. Watch this website and start saving up your money. zackyoung

I repeat. pppeter

Email, Fax

Dear Brian,

I was glad to get that email from you, don't worry about it. Whatever fucked up shit came down between us, it doesn't matter anymore. People change, that's right. I figured you were off doing your own thing and didn't remember me. I've fucked over so many people, I don't expect anyone to give a shit. I've been in AA off and on for a couple of months, and they make you think about what you do, and so I'm better about not going over people's boundaries, like they say. I'm sorry for being a shithead a lot of the time back then. I make people into my dad, and then I have these big expectations that are just stupid. I wish I didn't do that, but I still do. I just fucked up this thing with a guy here in Portland, although I have to say the guy was as much of an asshole as me. I don't have anybody right now, and I get fucked up when I'm alone. I was clean for four months, but now I slipped and everything goes to hell when I'm using. So your letter came at a good time, because I've been feeling like nobody gives a fuck. I'm sleeping in my van right now because I don't have anywhere to live, and I'm getting tired of it. I was doing pretty good for a while there. I got married to this woman Elaine, and she's going to have my baby. I was with her for a while, and that was a good time in many ways, but I couldn't play it the way she wanted me to play it, so she kicked me out. That's over. She has a restraining order against me, which I deserve because it got kind of crazy toward the end. I don't know if you want to hear all this shit. You seem to think I'm somebody special, and you always did, no matter how much I fucked you over, which is why I loved you like I did. But it hasn't worked out that I'm so special. That's probably why I was such an asshole to you, because you thought I was so special, and I knew I wasn't, but I wanted to believe it, so I wouldn't let you have what you wanted, because I knew if you did that shit with me for real, it wouldn't be what you thought because I'm just another fucking asshole like all the others. But then it got fucked up between us anyway, and later I thought I was a total prick for not just giving you what you wanted, because you were so nice to me, and I should have given it to you, because it's probably the only thing I could have given you to thank you and show you that I cared. But I didn't, so I've always felt like an asshole. I sort of wanted to do it, you know. I was just scared that you'd think big deal, because let's face it, that's what happens. It's not like I've been a saint since I last saw you. I try not to let people have me because it always fucks me up, but then I don't keep jobs very well, and I need money, so I let people have me, just so I can get by, and so that I have something in my life. So I'm not scared of that shit anymore. I don't have big hopes about it. I still had big hopes about it when I was with you. I just thought if I waited until I had my shit together it wouldn't be like I'd wasted my life. Then that time you started to go for it, and I freaked out, I thought I blew it. I didn't have my shit together, and now I don't think I'll ever have my shit together, so I feel like an asshole for freaking out. I don't know why you wrote to me, and I'm trying to understand why. The day I got your letter I went to a meeting and told them about you, and asked them what they thought. I didn't tell them you tried to kill me because they wouldn't understand, but I told them almost everything else. Those people all think I'm a fuck up, because I slip all the time, so I don't really care what they think, but they said maybe I hadn't blown it with you, and that I shouldn't just blow you off, and that I should write you back, and be honest with you about my circumstances and my addiction and so on, and see what happens. So I'm trying to be honest with you, but that's not something I'm good at. I'm trying to think about this, and not just say if you still want me you can have sex with me again as long as you give me some money. I told them that's what I wanted to say, and they said that I should say that I love you, and I want to be with you, and not say the money part. Really, I don't care about the money part except that I have nothing right now.

So they said I should be honest with you, and that's pretty honest. Sometimes I think the people who go to those meetings aren't being real. It's not real to think you're going to say I love you for who you are and we should be together. I already blew that, and I'll be honest with you, I think the drugs are always going to be a problem for me. So what I'm thinking is I could come stay with you for a few days and just see what happens. I was thinking of driving down to LA anyway and trying to get some money out of these guys I know there. I guess I'll just drive down in a couple of weeks and call you, and if you want to see me, cool. If you want to have sex with me, that's cool, and if you feel like giving me some money afterwards, that's cool, but I'm not expecting it. You said you don't know what you want with me now, and I don't know what I want either, not just with you but about everything. I know I want to go score, and I can do that, that's easy. I know I want you to have sex with me, if you still want me, and you said you do. I don't live my life like it matters anymore. When I shoot dope, I don't think if I do too much I'm going to overdose. I do as much as I feel like it to get as high as I can. When I let some fucking asshole have me for money, I don't tell him what he can't do, I just go with whatever he wants, because it's bullshit otherwise. I got married because I wanted to be with Elaine, and she wanted that, and I went for it. If you're still into that weird shit, that's the way it is. If I'm going to let you have sex with me, then you have sex with me the way you want. if I don't wake up the next morning, that's the way it is. You were the nicest person to me I ever knew, and I just fucked you over left and right, thinking I had to protect something. There's nothing to protect anymore. I gave it a shot, and it's not happening. If you want me, you can have me. I used to be so into trying to understand myself, but now I just want to do things, and not understand them.

I'll talk to you,
Brad

Dear Brian,

I'm coming down to Los Angeles next Tuesday. I have something to do that night, and then I'll call you and come over. It's perfect because, check this out, I've got this plan where I can steal a shit load of crystal meth from this guy down there. He thinks I'm buying it to sell, but fuck him. I've got it all figured out. So anyway, it'll be cool because I'll just come stay with you, and he won't know where the fuck I am, and I'll have all this crystal meth for us to use. I used to believe in all that love yourself crap, and then I sort of got out of that, but this whole thing is working out so great, I can almost believe it again. I'm so fucking high. I hope you can read this. When I got your last letter, I had to go celebrate, and fuck those AA guys who say they're my friends. You don't know the bullshit I've had to put up with, about accepting that I'm a fucked up, helpless person. I started to believe it, so thanks for reminding me that I'm cool. Yeah, I haven't gotten fat, Brian, don't worry. I'm fucking skinny as hell, but I could still go score with some guy right now, if that answers your question. I've got no problem getting guys to pay for it, as long as they don't give a shit about the tracks. I can still pass for really young. I bullshit guys that I'm fourteen all the time, so you don't have to worry about that, and I'm not going to worry about it either, because sometimes I can get really depressed about what I've done to myself, and I'm so sick of feeling like I blew all the shit that you used to think I was going to do with my life. You used to say I was going to be a great person, but I haven't done anything in a long time except try to get through every fucking day without killing myself. I tried to kill myself twice last year, if you want to know. The second time I almost did, and I used to be sorry it didn't work, but now I'm excited. Maybe I won't blow this thing with you. I feel like I have a chance. I've fucked up every good situation I've ever been in, and I decided that was because they were all bigger assholes than me, but you're not an asshole, and you know my problems, so maybe you won't be disappointed, because everybody's always so fucking disappointed with me. If you want to know, I was planning to steal that crystal meth and do all of it to kill myself, so this is great timing on your part. Thanks for giving me another chance. If I blow this, then that's it. You can go killer on me, and I won't even care. It would be better if you went killer on me than if you threw me out like everybody else has. Hey, I'm just fucking high. You're going to hear from me soon anyway, so I'll sign off.

Later,
Brad

Dear Brian,

Thanks for writing me back. It was a weird email, but I'm not going to worry about it. You just seem totally different. It seems like you're not the same person anymore, but you're right that my memory sucks. I'm different too. I think I'm better, but that's up to you. Anyway, you explained it, and we're cool. I'm sorry I got pissed off. I just had this idea in my head that you'd send me the money and I'd buy the bus ticket, but I don't blame you for thinking I'd use it to score. You're probably right. Ever since my van got stolen, I've been pretty on edge, so anyway I'm sorry again. So go ahead and buy me a bus ticket, and tell me when to be on it. If you don't mind driving me to that dealer guy's place, that'd be cool, since I'm not going to have wheels. I won't get you involved. You can just wait in the car. Anyway, I'm sorry about what shit I wrote that pissed you off. I was just jonesing, but a guy up here traded me dope for my ass, so it's cool. He said he had a really good time with me, so you don't have to worry about being disappointed with how I look now, if you're worried about that. Don't stop believing in me, Brian. It was just a bad day.

Thank you.
Brad

Dear Brian,

I guess you know by now that I didn't make it down there. I fucked up, okay? What do you expect? That's why I want to come down there and see you, because I'm a fucking mess on my own. I'll do whatever you say. If you send me another ticket, I won't sell it. I swear on my life. Please write me back. I love you. Do you know how hard it is for me to say that?

Brad

Brian,

Your email got me really pissed off. I wasn't going to write you back, but I thought about it, and I feel like I don't have a choice. I've really, really fucked things up here, not that you give a shit obviously. So yeah, whatever you fucking want. I'm just worried you don't love me anymore, because you haven't written that in a while, and that's all I've got to live for right now. So if you could just tell me that you do, that would be cool. I'll probably come anyway, but that would help, because I am kind of scared. You're getting pretty heavy on me, and I don't really have a problem with that, but the whole thing for me is that you love me, and if you don't anymore, then I don't know what the fuck to do. If you love me, I'll do fucking anything you want, don't you know that? I fucking swear. I don't know what you want me to say about your rules. I feel like I don't know what answers you expect, and I'm bad when I don't know what people want, because I always make the wrong decision, if it's up to me, but I guess you're saying I have to answer or you won't bring me down there and give me money and all that, so here you go. (1) Fine with you making a reservation so I won't be able to sell the ticket. I won't even get off the bus to take a shit, okay? The thing is I don't have any ID except for fake ID, so make the reservation or ticket or whatever for Thaddeus Stroh. It's a long story. (2) You already know all of that, so I don't get what the problem is. (3) I think it's really unfair of you to ask me that, because you know how hard it is for me. I told you I love you. All I can say is that the only person I've said that about is my wife. You make me feel like I'm important. I'd be upset if you were dead. If someone fucked you over, I'd fuck them over. I've jacked off thinking about you holding me in your arms and telling me the kinds of things you said in your letters a while back. I don't know what else to say. I'm going to come down there and be with you even though it scares the shit out of me, and part of me is worried you're going to kill me. I mean I'm not really worried, but you know what I mean. That's a big fucking sacrifice on my part, so I guess that must mean I love you. (4) The crystal meth deal's not going to happen now probably, because I sort of fucked it all up, so you don't have to worry about that. (5) I ask myself that question every fucking day. I don't think I'm worth shit. You're the one who thinks I'm so great. So I don't know how to answer that question, because it seems like a trick question to me, but then I can be really paranoid. I'm worth all this shit because I'm your friend, and because I'm going to let you do shit to me that I would never let anybody else do, and because you probably couldn't get anybody else to do that shit with you, and because I'm great looking like you said, okay? (6) I already told you that you can have any kind of sex you want to me, but, if you don't mind, I don't want to talk about the details anymore. Yeah, whatever you want, Brian. Go for it. I've been in jail enough times that I think I can deal with whatever you're talking about. Remind me to tell you sometime about the shit I went through in jail, because you'd probably really get off on it. Imagine someone who looks like me in jail, and figure it out. (7) You don't have to worry about me taking off, as long as I have my dope, and you have a TV and maybe a VCR. I don't care if you look different. Did you get fat or something? I don't care what you look like. You know that. So does that answer your rules? Now get me the fucking ticket, Brian, so we can be together. No offense.

Brad

Dear Brian,

You're going to be pissed off, but I have to change the plan a little. Just read this and you'll see why this has to happen, and why it'll be great for both of us. I fixed it so I could see that dealer guy after all, but he can't do it on Monday night, so I changed the bus ticket for a different day, and I'll call you from a pay phone near their place when I'm finished with the deal, because you shouldn't have to hassle with it anyway, and it's safer for both of us if I deal with it myself. So I'll call you, and don't be pissed off, okay?

Brad

Brian,

I'm faxing you because this guy won't let me use the phone or give you the phone number here. Like I said on your machine, I fucked up. This guy knows some guys who I sort of fucked over back in Portland, and they want $5000, and obviously I don't have it. I told him you could cover the money, but he's not letting me leave until he gets it. I'm scared, Brian. You've got to fucking help me. He's saying he's going to kill me if he doesn't get the money. This guy named Harold is going to call you, and will you please pick up the phone and talk to him, because he'll arrange the whole thing. I told him you'd do this, and you have to come through for me, or I'm dead. I'm sorry about this shit, but I don't know what else to do. I'll fucking owe you big time, if you do this for me. Come on, man. Please please please. Harold will call you tonight. I love you. Help me.

Brad

Brian,

Thank you, thank you, thank you. Harold is going to call you when he finishes doing something he has to do in a couple of hours. Thank you, thank you. You're the only good thing that's ever happened to me. Nobody else would do this for me, I know that. It'll be worth it, I swear.

Brad

Brian,

Fuck you. What the fuck is up with you sending that weird guy over to do our business? You don't even care enough to fucking come yourself? You want to have some asshole check me out for you? That guy was a fucking prick, so don't believe anything he says, okay? After the mean, evil shit he said to me last night, you deserve what happened. You're the biggest asshole I've ever known. You say you love me, but all you want is my fucking body for your sick sex bullshit. You've turned in such an asshole that you need some creepy guy to check me out and make sure I'm still good enough for you? I don't know what he told you, but I'm sure it was bullshit. Yeah, so I look wasted and skinny and shit right now. What do you fucking expect? It's me. That's all that matters, right? I was totally going to let you do all that weird shit to me, you know. That's how fucking desperate I am, because I thought you'd love me if I let you do that, because I do love you, you asshole. You've gotten me so confused, I don't know what to think anymore, but I just want to tell you that I had nothing to do with what happened with Harold. Yeah, I set it up for him, and he was supposed to give me part of the money, but he fucked me over just like he fucked you over, I swear. I was going to share it with you. I know you don't believe me. Now I'm much more fucked than you. You have money and a place to live, and I have nothing. I had to go down to Santa Monica Boulevard and sell my ass just to get a place to crash. I'm sorry you lost the money, and that I didn't stand up for you, but I've got nothing and now I'm stuck here, and this guy won't buy me drugs, and I'm sick. So I'm going to ask you if you'd please lend me some money so I can get high and go back to Portland. I think you owe me after all the mean shit your fucking friend said to me. You think that didn't hurt? I'm at some guy named Larry's place, but I don't think I can stay here past tonight because he's sick of my shit already. I know you don't want to have anything to do with me, and you probably don't even want to do that weird sex shit anymore, and I don't deserve your pity, but I'm asking you this one last favor, and then I'll fucking leave you alone. Fax me, okay? Be cool.

Brad

Dear Brian,

Yeah, that sounds cool. Thanks. I'm still totally cool with the sex stuff, I told you that. I'm up for it. I was just pissed off. I didn't mean it, you understand. I totally agree that I'm not as cute right now and the drugs are a big problem and that it can't be like it was before and I'll be more like your slave or whatever and you can pimp me out to other guys again and all that shit. That's all cool. How about this, though? Just read this and see what you think? I don't really want to live in LA anymore. If you could give me enough money to fly to Portland, and stay in a motel there for a couple of weeks, then that would be the best thing for me. Because Elaine lives there, and I think if I can get there, and get a job, and prove to her that I've got my shit together, she might give me another chance, and I'd be near my kid when it's born. I've been thinking that might really be the thing that would make me get my shit together. I know you hate me now, but I was just thinking if we could go back to that thing before about your rules and all that, and I could stay with you for maybe a week, and do whatever the fuck you want, and I can just be your whore and pretend I don't know you, and that you don't know me or whatever, like you said. You can pimp me out that week as much as you want. Maybe at the same time we're doing all that, I could kick drugs, so when I go to Portland, I'll be in good shape. I've kicked a hundred times and it never takes more than a week, and if you want to see me suffer, then you will. Doesn't that sound sort of perfect? You can tie me up, like you were saying, and do whatever the fuck you're going to do, and that way I won't be able to escape and go score at the same time. That's a really perfect plan, isn't it? So what do you say? Fucking great, right? I'm excited. I don't know why I didn't think of this before.

Brad

Brian,

Fuck you. No offense. Okay, I've been an asshole, and I've lied to you, but my life is fucked up right now, and I'm not at my best. What happened to all that shit about me being so great and brilliant, and the most important person you've ever known? Were you lying to me? How can say that shit you wrote? You're wrong if you think you understand me. I don't have a death wish, and I don't see your fucking logic about your violent sex thing and my death wish being a marriage of fate or whatever. I'm asking you, as your friend, not to go this way, okay? If you want to pretend to do it or whatever, and fuck me up a little, that's cool, and I get off on that in my own way, because I do hate myself, you're right about that. But you're scaring the shit out me, okay? You're just tripping out on your fantasy, right? Yeah, it's cool that we'll finally get it together. I'm sure you've got a million things you want to do to me, and I'm very cool with that, and I'll probably love it, okay? I have problems too, and I dig sex, and I've been known to feel right about being treated like shit, and I deserve that, and I've gotten off on it, and it's you, so I'll definitely get off on that, but don't go crazy, because you know I don't have a choice here. What else am I going to do? I've got nothing, and I have to go through with it, and I will, because I don't fucking believe that you mean it. I know when I'm with you, you'll remember why you thought I was great, and I'll remember too. I'll stay with you forever if you want. I swear to fucking God. That plan about Portland was just an idea. I don't have to do that. I could love you, and be with you, because when I think about it, I really do love you more than anyone ever in my whole life, even my wife. How about this? Remember you thought I was going to be a great person? Let's do that. I'll live with you, and go back to school. I think that's a great idea. I've been wanting to get back into school for a long time. So let's do it this way. We'll do the sex thing, and anything goes for as long as you want, that's cool, and then we'll both feel really good, and afterwards it will be like it was when we used to know each other, and I'll feel like I finally paid you back for being so great to me, and everything will be cool. It will be like my life never went to shit. Okay? I think that sounds perfect.

Brad

Brian,

Maybe I'm dense, but I don't understand your fax. I've been doing speedballs with Larry and this other guy, so that's probably why. I understand the thing that you're different now. You keep saying that. Are you saying you changed your name or Brian isn't your real name? I don't give a fuck. I don't know what you mean about the website thing. I don't know what you're talking about. You mean when those guys used to write reviews about our bullshit? I never really understood your whole thing about that. I'm high, Brian. I don't give a shit. Let's just fucking go for it, okay? I have to get the fuck out of here. Larry's pissed off about you faxing me and he's getting bored of me. I'm sure whatever you're talking about is cool. If you don't want to pay for a taxi, I'll just take the bus over to your place. I owe this guy who bought the drugs a fuck tonight, but I'll come over tomorrow. If you're not there, I'll just wait. See you tomorrow. I love you.

Brad

Zack,

Okay, you're not Brian. You're that guy who came to Harold's house. You wrote all the letters and faxes. I get it.

You have to admit it's pretty fucked up. No offense, but I don't believe your thing about how famous I am on that website and all that shit. Come on. I can't check it out because Larry won't let me touch his computer, and he won't check it out for me because thinks it's a joke. So what you're saying is all the shit we've been writing about stays the same except you're not Brian? I'll be honest with you. I don't give a fuck about Brian. I thought he was a fucked up asshole, but I'm desperate right now so I just said what he wanted me to say so I could get some money and a place to live for a while. If you're like him, then what I said goes for you too. If you want me to say I love you, cool. If you'll help me out, I love you, okay? I'm being honest. I just don't know what you expect. You saw me. That's what I look like with my clothes on, and as far sex goes, I'm always up for anything if the money's right. There's pretty much nothing I haven't been paid to do already. I'm just worried that if it's true about the website bullshit, you're expecting some fucking huge thing. You saw me, so I guess you know I'm not some fucking model. I can tell for you sure I have a cute ass. That's something I know. Whatever guys think about me, they always say my ass is really cute. I'll say this about Brian. That fucker really liked me. I tried to work it like he wanted, but it was too much pressure. Are you like him? I mean that you think I'm so fucking great that I have to die because you can't stand feeling what I make you feel and all that? I can play that, but it kind of gets me depressed sometimes. So you need to have drugs around if you want to go that way. Brian was into trying to save me, and I'll be honest with you, it's not going to happen. I used to get that a lot, and I can play it, but don't start thinking it's really going to happen. You know that whole thing Brian used to say about me dying of cancer is true. I don't like to think about it, but it's a fact. I'll tell you about it when I see you. So I'm telling you I can't be saved, okay? You don't seem like you want to save me anyway. That shit you said about me at Harold's was fucking cruel. I don't let things get to me, but that really shit fucked with my head. I was impressed. Is that what you're into? I can get off on that if the money's right. So what do you think about what I was saying before about hooking up with you for a while until I get clean and save some money so I can go back to Portland and be around my kid? I'm just saying that's something to think about. Maybe I'll fall in love with you and I can just stay with you. It's interesting what you said about how a serial killer almost killed you once. I guess I can relate to that. So we have a lot in common like you said. Guys usually get bored of me after a while, but maybe you won't. That's because they always want to know me and help me and shit. I think if it was just for sex, you wouldn't get bored. Brian said he never got sick of me. I would have stayed with him if he didn't try to kill me. You can relate to that, I guess. I'm not saying I wouldn't let you kill me if you're into that. I'm going to die anyway, right? It's true what I wrote before that I don't have any hopes anymore. I guess my kid is the only thing I'm living for, to be honest with you. But it wouldn't shock me if Elaine already got an abortion. She won't talk to me, so I don't know. I'm just saying I'm cool with it all. I just did a speedball so that's why I'm writing such a long fax. I'll shut up now. So I'll be standing on that corner like you said, and you pick me up, and we'll go from there, and I trust you. You said 7 pm but let's make it later like 11 pm because I have a couple things I need to do. I feel better now. Yeah, this is going to be fucking cool. I'm excited. See you in a while.

Brad

Site 2

Review #1

Escort's name: Brad

Location: West Hollywood

Age: 18?

Month and year of your date: April 2002

Where did you find him? friend

Internet address: unknown

Escort's email address: unknown

Escort's advertised phone number: I called 323-660-6555

Rates: $300

Did he live up to his physical description: yes, but . . .

Did he live up to what he promised? yes

Height: 5′11″?

Weight: 130 lbs?

Facial hair: no

Body hair: little

Hair color: blond

Eye color: blue
Dick size: 6″
Cut or uncut: cut
Thickness: thin
Does he smoke? not with me
Top, bottom, versatile: not sure
In calls/out calls/not sure: in calls
Kisser: not sure
Has he been reviewed here before? yes
Rating: A+
Hire again: sure
Handle: sandman808
Submissions: two
URL for pics: unknown

Experience: I have a somewhat unusual fetish. Give me a young guy with a cute face and well formed balls, and I'm a satisfied customer. Height, weight, race, hairy, smooth, cut, uncut, I don't care. I sound easy to please, but I'm very picky. To most guys, balls are balls, but perfect balls in a perfect sac on a body that has a truly cute face is a rare thing, and finding a cute guy into surrendering them is not a simple thing. I've had my best success in fetish chat rooms where there's less prejudice against men with highly particular tastes like myself. It was in one of these chat rooms that I got a tip on a young escort named Brad. A fellow chatter whose taste in young guys is similar to mine suggested I try Brad, whom he had found to be a very satisfactory scat bottom. He said that making arrangements with Brad was very unusual, but that he was worth the trouble.

I phoned the number that the chatter passed along to me and spoke to a man who claimed to be Brad's manager. He refused to email me pictures of Brad, but my fellow chatter had assured me that Brad's face was very cute. Also, Brad's manager offered me a very reasonable price, claiming that Brad was in 'the testing phase' before he went 'public.' He said I would get a special preview rate in return for giving him feedback on Brad's performance. He said that he would need to be in the room while Brad and I had sex, but that he would merely observe us unless I requested his participation. Of course I thought all of this was quite bizarre, but I was intrigued enough to make a date with Brad for later that evening.

As Brad only does in calls, I drove to his (or his manager's) house. The manager, who introduced himself as Brian, answered the door and made me a drink. He said Brad was getting ready for me, and we talked for a while. When I politely asked how he and Brad met, he asked me if I knew this website. When I said I did, he casually mentioned that he and Brad were rather infamous on this site. Call me stupid if you like, but it was only then that I realized I was talking to the one and only Brian and would soon be having sex with the one and only Brad. I was a dedicated follower of that whole strange affair, so finding myself in this situation was unnerving to say the least. I had so many questions that I didn't know where to begin. Brian was very reluctant to answer them, saying that everything would be revealed when Brad went public, but he did assure me that most of what I had read about them was untrue, and that I was in no danger. He said Brad was simply rusty at the moment due to his time in prison and his brief marriage, and needed a tune up. Ultimately, my curiosity got the best of me, and I decided to take a chance and proceed with the date.

At one point, Brian left the room for a minute then returned to tell me that Brad was ready and waiting. So I hurriedly finished off my drink and followed him into the bedroom. My nervousness went away as soon as I saw Brad on the bed. He was naked apart from a long sleeve t-shirt and had his legs spread wide so I could get a good look at his freshly shaved balls Brad would almost have to be inhuman to live up to kind of hype he has received on this site, and I found him to be quite human. On the plus side, he has a very cute and androgynous face with long, flattering blond hair. His small, low hanging balls are beautifully formed, and the skin of his sac is very tender and rubbery and a divine shade of pink. (If you're very into balls, you might want to wait a week or two before you hire Brad, as I gave them a quite working over.) His ass doesn't have a lot of meat on it, but it's soft and easy on the eyes and smells wonderful. On the negative side, Brad is not what I would call responsive. I remember that in his old set of reviews, he was described as hyper and chatty with unusual nervous tics, and in my experience he was anything but. He also refused to take off his shirt, which made me wonder why. He could stand to gain 10 or 15 pounds, and a visit to a tanning salon wouldn't do him any harm. His cock is rather small and thin, even when hard, and he was unwilling or unable to come. None of this was a problem for me since I require cooperation rather than response, but his extreme passivity and physical flaws could tax others' patience. There was much discussion in the past about Brad's real age. I was shown a driver's license that put Brad's age at 18, and frankly he looked at least 18 if not a year or two older. My guess is that prison and drugs have taken a toll. Whatever his real age, he doesn't seem like jailbait if he ever did.

I won't go into great detail about the sex, but Brad's balls were very accomodating. I met no resistance from him at any time and they accepted the full range of my attentions from a worshipful tongue bath to hard squeezes and bites to some bruising punishment. Watching his cute face go through its range of emotions was very hot, and knowing he was the legendary Brad made it even more special.

Afterwards, Brian quizzed me in the living room and revealed a little more information. He didn't specifically answer my questions about his much discussed intentions to kill Brad, but he did say that there were no limits to what Brad would do for a price. I will say that Brian seemed a much more cold, heartless man than I had imagined based on his posts in the old set of reviews. I saw no sign that he was in love with Brad or felt any affection towards him whatsoever. He was also a much younger and more attractive man than I had pictured, although I don't think his age and physical appearance has ever been discussed here. After about a half hour of discussion, I paid him and left. Overall, I would say it was a memorable experience for many reasons, and I'll be curious to see what others think.

You: I'm in my early 60s, average looking, and could lose a few pounds.

Webmaster's message: I debated for a week before posting this review. I confirmed the reported activities with sandman808 and with the person claiming to be Brian. I have decided to allow reviews of Brad to be posted for the time being contingent on my being able to make follow up confirmations both with the reviewers and either Brian or Brad. Like many of you, I am curious to get to the bottom of this saga, but be aware that reviewers are on a very tight leash. After confirming this encounter with Brian, I received the following response from him.

Brian's response: First of all, I'm very disappointed in sandman808. Our gentleman's agreement was that he would not post a review. I didn't think I had to go far as to have clients sign a confidentiality form, but I realize now that I should have done this. Also Brad's cock isn't huge, but it is average sized and very pretty. He didn't take off his shirt because he wasn't asked to. Brad's nervous tics are history thanks to a medication he takes. He can very responsive if the client requires it. If he was quiet with sandman808, it's because was concentrating on his client's needs. I will be placing escort ads for Brad within the next two weeks. At that point, he will be open to the public. Yes, we are the legendary Brian and Brad.

Review #2

Escort's name: Brad
Location: West Hollywood
Age: maybe 19
Month and year of your date: March 2002
Where did you find him? bareback.com
Internet address: none
Escort's email address: none
Escort's advertised phone number: none
Rates: none
Did he live up to his physical description? no
Did he live up to what he promised? oh, yeah
Height: not sure
Weight: thin

Facial hair: none
Body hair: practically none
Hair color: blond
Eye color: blue, I think
Dick size: 5"?
Cut or not: cut
Thickness: none
Does he smoke? yes
Top, bottom, versatile? bottom
In calls/out calls/not sure: not sure
Kisser: yes
Has he been reviewed before? I think so
Rating: depends
Hire again: not applicable
Handle: cumhose4you
Submissions: this is my third
URL for pics: no

Experience: I'm pretty sure I fucked Brad about two weeks ago. There was no money exchanged so I don't know if this qualifies as a review, but after reading sandman808's review, I thought you should hear what I have to say.

I was chatting one night on bareback.com when one guy in the chat room asked if anyone in the Los Angeles area felt like having a three-way with him and his boyfriend. He described his boyfriend as a young Leonardo di Caprio type who loved to get fucked raw and filled with cum. Four guys in the chat room including myself were interested, and he invited us over for a late night gangbang.

When I got there, one guy had already arrived and was doing crystal with the host. The host's boyfriend was playing a videogame by himself. As a recovered heroin addict, I can spot junkies a mile away. The boyfriend had the classic signs of advanced heroin addiction, nodding out, pinned pupils, and a long sleeved shirt even though the temperature was toasty. He was cute and trashy hot in the way young junkies can be, but saying he looks like Leonardo di Caprio is a stretch. A slightly cuter Kurt Cobain, maybe. I don't party anymore, so I played a videogame with the boyfriend while the other guys partied. The last two guys showed up after a while, and started partying with the first two. It was then that the host started telling us how he and his boyfriend had pulled off this major scam on this website. I realized pretty quickly that he meant the Brian and Brad thing, but the other guys didn't seem to know anything about it, and I kept my mouth shut. He said he and his boyfriend had broken up for while, but they'd reconciled recently and were planning a scam that would make the earlier one seem like nothing. He said his name was Brian and his boyfriend's name was Brad, and we should remember those names and check out this website in a couple of weeks. I thought he was spouting a load of crap, especially since his boyfriend kept calling him Zack then correcting himself. I forgot all about that part of the night until I read sandman808's review and remembered that guy from the old message board discussion who said he was in contact with Brad and had a profile on bareback.com. I checked the profile. The guy we tricked with had a different haircut and was a few pounds heavier, but it was the same guy, even down to the name Zack. I think this Zack character hooked up with Brad and they're both pretending he's Brian for whatever reason. I'd bet money on it. I don't want to get all conspiracy theory, but for all I know they could have killed the real Brian and taken his place. Has anyone heard from him in a while? After spending most of a night with these two scumbags, I think anything is possible.

Another thing. I'm a proud practitioner condom free sex, but I believe it's a choice that should only be made after weighing the benefits against the risks. In that spirit, I think anyone who considers hiring Brad should know he was the bottom for some highly unsafe sex that night. If he's not poz, I'm Princess Diana. If you're a top into raw sex and don't expect too much from your bottom, he is one helluva fuck. We screwed him so long and hard the bed literally broke and crashed to the floor. He had no problem being double penetrated, and his juicy gaping hole was really something to see. He does this cool trick where his ass swallows a load then blows the cum back in your mouth like a whale. He gave lousy head, but his throat was always open and hot and bottomless. I guess if you've gotten too caught up in the Brad and Brian thing and expect him to be some perfect twink, you're gonna be disappointed. But for raw sex, he's one of the cuter and more adventurous kids I've been with. But here's a piece of advice. Get right to the sex, do it, then get out. He and Brian are an arrogant, boring, shifty couple of guys.

You: I'm a 28 year old, masculine Hispanic/Asian bb top into gangbangs, public scenes, and general nastiness.

Webmaster's report: This review has been confirmed with cumhose4you and confirmed in part with the person calling himself Brian. They agree that sex happened as stated. Brian claims that cumhose4you partied as heavily as anyone else that night. He suggests that cumhose4you's statement that he is not Brian is the result of drug induced confusion or paranoia. I welcome all reliable third party confirmations or denials of cumhose4you's claims. Brian also stated that Brad is not a heroin user. I have just received the first official review of Brad, which I will post in the morning. It's an interesting and informative and unusual review. Lastly, Brian asked me to mention that he has placed listings for Brad's services on the following escort sites: americanmale.net, bareback.com, barebacksex.com, and rentboy.com. He asks that all potential clients of Brad consult these listings for fees and available services before contacting him.

Review #3

Escort's name: Brad

Location: Los Angeles

Age: 18 or 19?

Where did you find him: rentboy.com

Internet address: no

Escort's email address: listed as meetalegend@hotmail.com

Escort's advertised phone number: 323-660-6555

Rates: $2500 hr

Did he live up to his physical description? not completely

Did he live up to what he promised? not applicable

Height: maybe 5'9"

Weight: thin

Facial hair: no

Body hair: don't know

Hair color: blond

Eye color: greenish-blue

Dick size: unknown

Cut or uncut: unknown

Thickness: unknown

Does he smoke? unknown

Top, bottom, versatile? advertised as bottom

In calls/out calls/not sure: in calls

Kisser: unknown

Has he been reviewed here before? yes!!!

Rating: not applicable

Hire again: not applicable
Handle: hornynice
Submissions: a bunch
URL for pics: unknown

Experience: My mind was blown to learn that mere mortals like myself might get the chance to check out the holy Brad. It's funny how the mind works. Brad was never my type. I wouldn't have given a second thought to hiring him back in the old days. After everything that has been discussed and rumored since then, I'm even less hot to trot for him. But like someone wrote on the old Brad message board, this is one hell of a mystery story, and I'm obsessed with figuring out whodunit or maybe that should be whoisit.

Lo and behold, after reading sandman808's review, I was scrolling through LA escorts on rentboy.com yesterday hoping against hope when I saw a new listing for a Brad. There was no picture, but I guess that would be asking too much. His price was predictably outrageous and the activities he was available for were predictably extreme beyond extreme. Figuring that Brad would soon be booked up until the next century, I leapt for the phone and called the number in the listing. I left a message and my call was returned within a couple of minutes. I spoke to Brian, which was a mind boggler in itself, and booked an hour with Brad for that afternoon. I didn't tell Brian this, but I really just wanted to meet Brad and ask him some questions.

I was met at the door by Brian. I had no mental image of what he would look like, but I was surprised that he was a total stud muffin. I don't know if this is his standard policy, but I was required to sign a written agreement that I wouldn't reveal certain things: I couldn't physically describe Brian in any review that I might write. I couldn't reveal the location where the date had taken place. I could take no photographs or video of any kind either inside or outside the house. And there were a few other things. I'll be trying to follow the rules as I write this. I was worried that Brian might not let me be alone with Brad, but it seemed to be no problem. He asked what I was going to do with Brad, and I said I wanted to let nature take its course. That was the extent of our conversation. He asked to be paid in advance, and then directed me to the bedroom. I was incredibly nervous, but I think I did a good job of masking it as excitement.

When I walked in the bedroom, Brad was sitting on the edge of the bed. He was dressed in a black long sleeved t-shirt that had the name of some rock band on the chest. He had on baggy, worn out blue jeans and dirty white socks. He has a very cute face, as the first reviewer mentioned, but he is very thin and his skin color is unhealthy. I guess I must have been staring because he smiled and shrugged as if to say, yes it's the famous me. He seemed shy but pleasant enough, so I decided to be honest and tell him that I didn't want to have sex but rather ask him some questions. From his reaction, I had the feeling he was relieved by this. He sat silently for a few seconds, then said that was okay with him so long as I didn't tell Brian. He seemed worried that Brian might find out, but I assured him I wouldn't say anything and he seemed fine after that. Of course this raised the question for me whether he was being held there against his will, but I didn't ask and can't say for sure.

I sat on the bed next to him and asked questions until my time was up. Here's what I learned. Is he aware of the discussion and rumors about him on the internet? Answer: He's heard about it, but hasn't seen it. He only saw some of the earlier reviews. Is or was he married and, if so, is his wife pregnant? Answer: He's married but his wife is getting a divorce. His wife was pregnant but recently aborted the child. Was he in prison? Answer: Yes. Did he communicate with people on the outside via email was he was in prison? Answer: No. Did he set fire to builtlikeatruck's business? Answer: Yes, but builtlikeatruck deserved it. Why? Answer: None of your business. Did or does he wanted to be killed? Answer: It's a stupid question. Why is it a stupid question? Answer: Try to kill me and you'll find out. How old is he? Answer: 18. Is the man in other room Brian? Answer: Ask him. Does he have a neurological disorder? Answer: He did, but he's on a new medication and it's better now. Why did he reunite with Brian? Answer: He didn't have anywhere else to go. Why does he let men have extreme sex with him? Answer: For money and because it makes him feel important. Any message to his fans? Answer: Hire me.

If you want my overall impression of Brad, I would say

he's a much chillier and more remote boy than I had expected. I remember in the old reviews he was described as hyperactive and easily distraught, but he is far from that. He seems sour, bored, and cynical. Much used to be made about how young he looked, but he doesn't look a day under 18 or 19. I realize he has been through a lot in the past months, but it's hard to believe that he could have been mistaken for 14 less than a year ago. I remember in the old reviews that his hair was dyed blond but his hair looks naturally blond to me. I think his eyes might be a different color too, but I'm not sure. He answered my questions, but when I pressed him for details, he clammed up. Maybe he didn't think it was any of my business, or maybe he didn't know the details. I have serious doubts that this is the same boy. I wonder if there's anyone out there who hired Brad at the beginning and would consider checking him out and letting us know.

You: I'm 27, average looking. I like the company of escorts. Sex is less important to me than feeling like we've made a connection.

Webmaster's report: This review has been confirmed with hornynice. Brian has confirmed that hornynice hired Brad but refutes his claims of an interview. According to Brian, the date consisted of hornynice giving Brad a bloody nose and lip then licking the blood off his face while masturbating. Brian declined to let me speak with Brad directly.

Because of this and hornynice's history of legitimate reviews on this site, I have decided to print the review.

Message from bizeeby: I reviewed Brad in July of last year. Some of you may recall my account of our disastrous date in a hotel near LAX. I'm curious as to whether the Brad in these new reviews is the same Brad. I live in Pittsburgh, but travel to Los Angeles on business four times a month. I will be in Los Angeles for three days next week. Brad's current fee is way out of line with my budget. However, if one or more of you would be willing to help finance this meeting, I would be willing to hire Brad and submit a review. I can be reached at bizeeb7@yahoo.com.

Message from llbean: I hired Brad in June, 2001. I believe mine was the second or third review. I have no interest in getting anywhere near him, but if someone wants to sneak a camera into the bedroom, take a decent shot of him, and post it online, I would be happy to confirm or deny that it's the same boy.

Review #4

Escort's name: Brad
Location: LA.
Age: 18

Month and year of your date: April 2002

Where did you find him? barebacksex.com

Internet address: I don't know

Escort's email address: I forget

Escort's advertised phone number: 323-660-6555

Rates: $7000/3 hrs

Did he live up to his physical description: yes

Did he live up to what he promised? amazingly, yes

Height: 5′10″ or so

Weight: skinny

Facial hair: not

Body hair: not

Hair color: blond

Eye color: I forget

Dick size: small

Cut or uncut: cut

Thickness: not

Does he smoke? yes

Top, bottom, versatile? bottom

In calls/out calls/not sure: in call

Kisser: ?

Has he been reviewed before? yes

Rating: excellent

Hire again: doubt it

Handle: bones4puppy

Submissions: this is my first

URL for pics: not.

Experience: This is my first review. I wasn't aware of this site or the back story on this escort until today. The only reason I'm submitting this review is because I was asked to by the escort's manager. It's simple. I saw a profile in the escort section of barebacksex.com for an 18 year old superstar bottom (Brad). I thought superstar meant he'd been in porn videos, but I'm not that familiar with porn. I liked his stats and attitude, but his rates were so high that I thought it was a typo. I called the number and talked to a guy who turned out to be the escort's roommate and manager. He said the rates were high because Brad's services are geared toward wealthy clients with extreme fantasies. He said clients seeking bargain quickies should look elsewhere.

I have a very extreme fantasy that I've never been able to realize. Ever since my high school days back in the Sixties, I've had a thing for teenaged boys with broken legs. I still remember the day a cute freshman showed up at school walking on crutches with his leg in a cast. It was an epiphany for me. I began to fantasize that I had broken his leg. I imagined I was hitting it with a baseball bat. I imagined the sound of the bones snapping and how the leg would twist in impossible directions. When he was immobilized, I imagined yanking down his pants and underwear then eating out his ass and raping him while he cried in pain. I still obsess privately about acting out this fantasy with a boy who looks like him. I'm always in search of escort bottoms have that boy's hippie pothead look and slim, wiry build.

I shared my fantasy with the escort's manager not really expecting him to accomodate me. To my surprise, he quoted me a price. I said you realize your boy's going to be out of commission for a while. He said he understood. I thought he was fucking with me but I went ahead and set up an appointment. When I showed up for the appointment, the manager had me sign a confidentiality agreement and asked for the money up front. I've had bad experiences with up front payments and refused. He said either I paid first or the appointment was cancelled. I said I would pay up front if I could see the escort. He agreed and the escort entered the room. I thought he was very cute, and he even had the kind of long hair I love. Even in his clothes, I could tell he had the kind of long, slim legs and flat, no-big-deal ass that drives me crazy. So I paid the manager.

The three of us partied for a while until the escort was fucked enough to do the scene. He was clearly too out of it to realize what was happening to him, but I asked the manager a couple of times if I should stop, and he said I could keep going. I ended up breaking both of his ankles, both knees, and both of his legs in several places. His ass more than lived up to my expectations. It was pale and almost homely in the hottest way. It just screamed, I'm a straight, asexual virgin teenager's ass. His hole was big and loose and very giving. Eating him out was heaven, and raping him almost made me explode. I would say that he and the sex were perfect except for one thing. The agreement I signed prevents me from saying this, but I'm going to say it anyway because I need to get this off my chest. At one point toward the end of the appointment, the roommate quoted me a price to kill the escort. I thought he was kidding at the time, but now that I know a little about the back story, I think he might have been serious. Apart from that strange moment, it was an unreal and unforgettable night.

You: a 56 yr old high school teacher

Webmaster's report: This review is confirmed with bones4puppy and Brian. Brian's response follows. We're getting dangerously close to the removal of these and all future reviews of Brad. Consider this a warning.

Brian's response: I have several points I want to make. First of all, I neither confirm nor deny bones4puppy's claim that I offered him a price to kill Brad. I don't want to spoil the fun. That's for me to know and for you to find out. Second, I didn't realize that bones4puppy was unfamiliar with my and Brad's history. I just assumed that anyone willing to pay Brad's high fee would already be a fan. This was my mistake, and it won't happen again. All future clients of Brad will be required to take a Brad and Brian quiz before any appointment is confirmed. Brad and I have no intention of wasting him on guys who don't fully appreciate what they're being given. Brad is making huge sacrifices and it's very important to him (and me) that his sacrifices mean something. He wants his clients to fully appreciate the tremendous honor of acting out their wildest fantasies with a true legend. It's very disturbing to us both that a know-nothing like bones4puppy was given such a tremendous privilege. Third, because so many of you want to experience Brad but cannot afford his fee, I have decided to offer the option of having a more affordable if limited encounter with Brad. Beginning today, for a fee of $300 dollars, Brad's fans can spend a vanilla hour with Brad on a first come, first served basis. You can look at him. You can touch and lick him above the waist. You can smell but not touch his genitals and ass. You can masturbate and come on his face or in his mouth. Those are the rules, and they are not negotiable. Fourth and last, clients should know that at the current time Brad can not walk or stand without assistance, and his legs are in casts. His mouth, genitals, and ass remain fully functional and available to satisfy your every desire.

Review #5

Escort's name: Brad!
Location: West Hollywood
Age: advertised as 18
Month and year of your date: April 2002
Where did you find him? this website

Internet address: I don't think so

Escort's email address: meetalegend@hotmail.com

Escort's advertised phone number: 323-660-6555

Rates: $300 an hour

Did he live up to his physical description? partly

Did he live up to what he promised? yes

Height: tallish

Weight: too thin

Facial hair: none

Body hair: pubes

Hair color: dark blond

Eye color: blue

Dick size: maybe 5 or 6 inches

Cut or uncut: cut

Thickness: not very

Does he smoke? I don't know

Top, bottom, versatile: bottom

In calls/out calls/not sure: in

Kisser: I couldn't tell

Has he been reviewed before? yes

Rating: for me, great

Hire again: no

Handle: sososogreat

Submissions: I think four

URL for pics: http://hometown.aol.com/userpage/davidbriggs/

Experience: When I read that there was an affordable way to spend some time with Brad, I contacted Brian immediately to make an appointment. He was cordial and businesslike on the phone. He gave me what he calls his quiz. I had to answer ten questions about my knowledge of his and Brad's relationship. I didn't become a fan until the Brad message board, so I got a few answers wrong, but apparently I just squeaked by because he gave me an appointment. I wanted to get off with Brad, of course, but I also hoped to get a photograph of him. Brian told me several times that there was no photography allowed, but I own a tiny digital camera that's barely bigger than my thumb, so I took a chance and brought it along concealed in one of my socks.

When I got there, Brian had me sign his contract and pay him. All I can say about him is that he's not what I expected at all. Before we went into the bedroom to meet Brad, he patted me down. Boy, was I sweating that, but luckily he didn't find the camera. I asked to use the bathroom and moved the camera into my left hand and concealed it in my palm.

Meeting Brad was intense, of course. We walked in the bedroom and there he was lying naked on his back in bed with two broken legs. He seemed like he was in a really bad mood, but Brian said it was just the pain from his broken legs. Like one of the reviewers said, he doesn't look as young as I thought he would. He's very skinny (you can see his ribs and everything), but that didn't surprise me. His cock isn't so big (when it's soft at least), but it has a nice mushroom head (circumcised, if you're wondering). His best feature is his face which has what I would call a Eastern European poor boy look. If you've seen the videos of that Czech porn company Man's Best, you'll get the picture. He had a swollen lip and bruised (broken?) nose and bloodshot eyes, so it's hard to judge, but I couldn't really understand how he could have made Brian and whoever else get so obsessed with him. He is cute in a weird way, but I expected something else. I wanted to hear what his voice sounded like so I said something like, Hi Brad, it's an honor to meet you, but he didn't say anything. He didn't a word the whole time I was there.

I was hoping Brian would leave the room, but he sat in a chair and started reading a copy of Unzipped Magazine. That made me feel really self-conscious, but I tried not to think about it. I wasn't turned on at all, but what's that old saying? — just close your eyes and think of England? I didn't close my eyes but I thought about all the things I'd read about him and just tried to think of it as an honor. Mostly I was just thinking how I could take a picture. While I was thinking about that, I felt Brad up a little and sniffed him and put on a show that I was hot to trot. Photographing him seemed impossible, but then I got really lucky.

Brian's cell phone rang, and he answered it. I could see he wanted to talk privately, so I smiled at him to let him know I was cool and having a good time. He said he had to take the call and would be back in a minute, then left the room. I quickly aimed the camera at Brad's face and took a shot. Brad looked right at the camera then looked at me with a confused expression. Brian returned at that very moment, and I quickly hid the camera. I was terrified that Brad was going to say something to Brian, but he just kept looking at me. I tried to give him a look like, Please don't say anything, and I don't know what he thought, but he didn't say a word about it. I wanted to get out of there, but I knew I had to get off to make it seem like I had gotten what I paid for. So I pulled my cock out and imagined my all time favorite Brad fantasy—him being gang raped and hung by his neck in prison—and looked down at his face. It worked. I shot off on his face and then cleaned myself and got out of there as fast as I could.

The picture I took of Brad isn't that great but you can see him clearly. I've put the picture on my homepage at http://hometown.aol.com/userpage/davidbriggs/ so you can check it out.

You: I'm a 22 year old physics major who doesn't need to buy escorts but likes to do it anyway.

Webmaster's message: I confirmed this review with sososo-great. Seeing as how he has a history of writing legitimate reviews on this site, I tend to believe him. Brian has refused to confirm this review and his following response presents his side of the story. Hopefully we have reached the point where the many questions about Brad can begin to be answered. I urge all of you who can confirm or deny Brad's identity to send me your reports, and I will post relevant and legitimate ones as they arrive.

Brian's response: This review is a bald faced lie. The picture on the reviewer's homepage is not a picture of Brad. I was in the room during this entire encounter watching closely and if any photograph had been taken, I would have known about it. You can thank this liar for the fact that I have cancelled all outstanding and future $300 appointments with Brad. This option is no longer available. This deceitful prick has ruined it for everyone. But just so you know, all future clients of Brad will be swept with a metal detector so don't even think about trying to sneak in a camera or tape recorder. Brad is available for serious, hardcore, committed admirers only.

Message from sandman808: I can't tell you if the boy in the picture on sososogreat's homepage is the 'real' Brad, whatever that means, but I can tell you that he is the boy I hired (see review #1). If you make an appointment with Brad, that's who you're going to get.

Review #6

Escort's name: Brad
Location: West Hollywood

Age: 18
Month and year of your date: April 2002
Where did you find him? your site
Internet address: none
Escort's email address: meetalegend@hotmail.com
Escort's advertised phone number: 323-660-6555
Rates: $300/hr
Did he live up to his physical description? absolutely
Did he live up to what he promised? absolutely
Height: 5′11″
Weight: 135 lbs.
Facial hair: smooth
Body hair: smooth
Hair color: blond
Eye color: hazel
Dick size: 6 inches
Cut or uncut: cut
Thickness: medium
Does he smoke? yes
Top, bottom, versatile: bottom
In calls/out calls/not sure: in calls only
Kisser: yes
Has he been reviewed before? yes
Rating: Excellent
Hire again: yes
Handle: damnstraight
Submissions: this is my first

URL for pics: no

Experience: I'm of the lucky guys who had a $300 appointment with Brad before the Brian guy stopped allowing them. I'm a huge fan of Brad. I've been into him since the very beginning. I'm a wiccan and have been casting spells to meet him for months. I credit my religion with my unbelievable luck and good fortune.

As a true fan, I've never expected Brad to be another Justin Timberlake or anything. I knew he wasn't a conventionally cute twink or porn star type. People seem to have forgotten that he started his career as a street whore. I knew he'd have a little wear and tear around the edges, and I wasn't disappointed in him at all. I wished he didn't have broken legs, but other than that I thought he was killer cute and killer sexy. I got hard the second I saw him and stayed hard the whole time. He got hard too, which meant a lot to me. I would have loved to taste his tender cock and feel his hot load splashing down my throat. His smooth white body was dreamy. I devoured his armpits and sucked his little nipples and gave his upper body a worshipful tongue bath. The Brian guy even let me give him a couple of hickeys, which was so nice. I snuffled around in his crotch like a dog just dying at the hot, potent odor. The real piece de resistance (sp?) was when Brian rolled him over so I could sniff his awesome ass. I'll never forget that sweet young ass smell or the sight of those soft, innocent white cheeks and that long, tantalizing, hairless crack. I would have sold my mother into slavery to bury my face in that ass and feel my tongue inside that warm, perfect body.

Brad was everything I'd dreamed about and everything I've ever wanted. I shot the biggest load of my life in his mouth. It was like I would never stop coming, and when he swallowed it, I lost my mind knowing that I was part of him. I will never forget Brad and what we did for as long as I live.

Webmaster's report: Review confirmed by phone with Brian and by email with damnstraight. Also, for those of you who might not have heard this already, David Barrows (better known to readers of this site as the escort Corey #3 of San Diego) plead guilty to the first degree murder of Kenneth Miller (Stevie Sexed). The San Diego Union newspaper reports that David Barrows and John Sperly (who is awaiting trial) murdered Kenneth Miller for the purpose of making a snuff video. Sperly is known within the amateur gay porn industry as Captain Sprinkle, producer and director of a series of videos with an SM theme. In return for his guilty plea, Barrows will not be charged in the murders of several other young San Diego males, including the escort known as Kevin, whose disappearance was discussed frequently in the first set of Brad and Brian reviews. Seeing as how the Brad and Brian saga and the murder of Stevie Sexed have always been intertwined, I thought it would be relevant to post this update here.

Message from bizeeb7: I was unable to raise the money to hire Brad while I'm in Los Angeles this coming week. I want to thank pppeter and goodnplenty for their offers to contribute. I did get a chance look at the picture on sosososgreat's homepage. It is not an accurate representation of the Brad I hired. There is a slight resemblance, mostly in the nose and in the general shape of the face, but there is no question in my mind. He is not the same boy. Hope that helps.

Review #7

Escort's name: Brad
Location: West Hollywood
Age: 18
Month and year of your date: May 2002
Where did you find him? a friend's recommendation
Internet address: unknown
Escort's email address: unknown
Escort's advertised phone number: 323-660-6555
Rates: $10,000/overnight
Did he live up to his physical description? yes
Did he live up to what he promised? yes
Height: 5′11″
Weight: 135 lbs.
Facial hair: none

Body hair: none
Hair color: blond
Eye color: hazel
Dick size: 6 inches
Cut or uncut: cut
Thickness: medium
Does he smoke? not with me
Top, bottom, versatile: bottom
In calls/out calls/not sure: In calls
Kisser: yes
Has he been reviewed before? yes
Rating: superb
Hire again: doesn't apply
Handle:
Submissions:
URL for pics: http://hometown.aol.com/userpage/davidbriggs/

Experience: For reasons that will become obvious, I must keep information about myself to a minimum. I can say that until approximately one year ago, I was in the medical profession. I was on the surgical staff of a well known and highly respected American hospital. I was forced into an early retirement as part of the settlement of a lawsuit against the hospital. I mention this portion of my background in order to help explain the particulars of my experience with the escort in question.

I have a friend who regularly employs the services of

escorts and swears by this website's advice and counsel. He knows my interests and tastes very well, and has been on the look out for an escort who might be willing to accomodate one extreme and difficult to realize fantasy of mine. He recently informed me about the existence of the escort Brad, whom he thought might be able to accomodate me. He directed me to a website where I could view a picture of the escort in question. Not only did I find his appearance more than satisfactory, but I happen to own an amateur porn video in which he performs, so I was already familiar with his body. Due to the stated prerequisite that men wishing to hire this escort have some foreknowledge of his history, and the fact that, apart from this single appearance in a video, I am ignorant on the subject, my knowledgeable friend endeavored to set up the appointment by assuming my identity. Considering the severity of my interests, I fully expected a negative response. I was startled when he informed me that the appointment had been made. The required fee, though substantial, was nonetheless lower than I had anticipated.

Upon arriving at the location where the appointment was to take place, I met first with the escort's agent. I had booked the escort for an overnight session, and we took some time to discuss the activities that would be taking place. I informed him then of my special needs in this regard and we made the appropriate arrangements. I initialed his contract, and he searched my person and medical bag for any hidden visual or audio recording equipment. Despite my fears that I might experience a last minute moral or ethical dilemma, I found myself instead in a state of unprecedented arousal.

After a period of debate with the agent, it was decided that my goals would be best achieved by transporting the escort into the kitchen. As has been discussed, the escort's legs are immobilized in casts. The agent and I carried the escort from the bedroom into the kitchen and lifted him into a sitting position directly over the sink. He was alert and in some discomfort, but was entirely cooperative. I should add that he was not informed at that time of the actions that would be taking place in order to minimize any panic or distress that might prevent him from achieving an erection.

My goals with the escort were two-fold—a benign sexual activity followed by a malignant final action and related sex act. For roughly the first hour of the encounter, I applied oral and tactile stimulation to his genitals and the immediately surrounding area. His penis began to stiffen and the testicles contracted. Their temperature rose dramatically, accompanied by the intensifying aroma of his activated tissues, flesh, and local internal organs. Despite what most laymen seem to believe, this aroma varies substantially in strength and quality from body to body, and this escort's scent was of a particularly attractive nature. I am not a poet, so I will not attempt to convey my reaction. My knowledge of human anatomy does not preclude a deep appreciation of sex, and I find it only enhances the experience for myself and my partners. In the case of this escort, there were extenuating factors as well. I had been quite aroused by his performance in the aforementioned video, and my senses were heightened by the presence of a body about which I had a long standing attraction and curiosity.

As my libidinal urges intensified, my expertise began a happy collaboration with my less cerebral instincts, and I increased my ministrations, inserted two digits easily into his anal cavity, and massaged his prostrate. My teeth and tongue then joined the frontal attack, gently but firmly stimulating his genitals into a state of readiness. I should add that my knowledge that the escort's impending orgasm would be the final such occurence of his life created a sense of anticipation and privilege that greatly heightened my pleasure. In laymen's terms, I alternated between sucking his cock and masturbating him, licking his testicles and perineum, and applying pressure to his prostrate gland until I recognized the physical symptoms of his arriving orgasm. I then inserted his penis between my lips and my mouth was quickly filled with three distinct expulsions of spermatosa. The flavor and volume of his orgasm were very pleasing and brought tears to my eyes.

The final and most significant phase of my experience then commenced. Based on advice from the escort's agent, a decision had been made to inform him of my intentions once his orgasm had been successfully accomplished. The escort's agent was convinced that he would welcome my actions. However, I was not surprised by his fearful and angry reaction, even as it caught his agent off guard. After a brief, violent, and ultimately futile struggle, the escort was secured by his agent. With no small difficulty, his arms were drawn behind his back and his wrists bound. He remained highly emotional, screaming expletives at his agent and begging me to reconsider. I had anticipated this reaction and found it arousing, but at a certain point a decision was made that it would be best to sedate him with an injection. He then grew relaxed and sufficiently disoriented that answering the simplest questions proved impossible.

We returned his body to a seated position over the sink. My heart rate was accelerated yet my hands remained steady as I washed and sterilized the escort's genitals, then injected a local anesthetic into his groin to numb the general area and further hamper his movements. I arranged the surgical instruments I would need on a clean dish towel. Pulling his testicles sac taut with my left hand, I began the operation. I cut deeply into the northernmost trunk portion of the sac. I quickly sliced horizontally through the trunk until the sac was separated from the escort's body. I laid it on the counter and set to work repairing the damaged and heavily leaking blood vessels. In conventional circumstances, precautions are taken to prevent the possibility of infection. Not only would this have been impossible to achieve under the conditions at hand, but the crudeness of the operation was a key component of my fantasy's enactment. The agent endeavored with some success to raise the level of the escort's consciousness with blows to his face and stomach. His attention was then directed to my actions. Upon registering the reality and consequence of his castration, he began to emit what I would describe as a wailing or mourning sound.

Using what might be described for reasons of brevity as a small blowtorch, I alternately cauterized damaged blood vessels and damaged the internal organs key to his sexual function. Flushing the area with tap water, I pulled the damaged organs into view and sliced them free, then cauterized the new wounds. The escort began vomiting, and lost control of his bowels, defecating into the sink. This pathetic reaction was everything I could have hoped, but I was able to complete my operation with some concentration, even as the urge to satisfy myself sexually grew almost uncontrollable. I cleaned the decimated cavity as best I could using the modest amount of sterilized water that I had brought along with me, then stitched together the remaining skin of his testicle sac which effectively closed the wound. No trace remained that a pair of testicles had ever existed in that spot. After allowing myself a moment of awe at what I had created, I quickly washed the fecal material from his anal region then gathered a few items from my medical bag as well as the severed testicle sac.

The escort's agent and I carried the semi-conscious young

man into the bedroom. We sat him down on the bed, and I emptied the contents of the testicle sac into his mouth then taped his mouth shut. While I undressed, the agent ordered the escort to position himself face down on the bed, and, after punching him violently about the head, he did as he was told. Let me drop my composure for a moment and try to convey the powerful effect of what I had accomplished. I (and others before me, to give credit where credit is due) had maimed, emasculated, desexualized, and demoralized an 18 year old boy to the point where his solitary value lay in his body's ability to gratify men's sexual urges and yet not only was that value severely diminished, but he himself was incapable of sexual gratification. No female would desire him again, nor would any gay male who was not aroused by the idea of causing him misery and contributing in some way to his death. As someone whose life had been dedicated to repairing and saving the wounded and ill, and who had been unfairly relieved of my career, this about face was a profound catharsis. The escort's death was now inevitable, warranted, and arguably humane, and my urge to kill him was tempered only by my arousal by his agent's promise that further torture and humiliation awaited him.

Now there was the matter of his ass, whose natural beauty and considerable erotic effect had preoccupied me since my initial introduction to it in the aforementioned video. In my years as a medical professional, I have witnessed and examined thousands of young male asses, some of them quite extraordinary examples of nature's genius, and I can say with some assurance that it measured up to the finest of them. Ultimately, I would say its inviting form more than any other factor saved the escort's life on that particular evening. When I could no longer bear the effect of so many conflicting feelings, I mounted the escort and raped him with as much force and violence as I was able to muster. While raping him, I asked the agent to remove the tape from the escort's mouth but not allow him to expel the testicles. I ordered the escort to chew and swallow his testicles. He declined to do so, either from confusion or disgust, but the agent threatened and delivered head and body blows that convinced him to do as he was told. He chewed the testicles and attempted unsuccessfully to swallow them, and it was this horrible and beautiful image which finally triggered my orgasm.

The appointment concluded with a gentleman's agreement between the agent and myself that I would serve as the escort's personal physician, remaining on call to treat his future injuries as they happen to arise. In return for my services, I will be allowed to gratify myself sexually with him as I wish during these house calls. I was asked by the agent to include this information in my review.

You:

Webmaster's report: I am posting this review for several reasons, despite the fact that I was unable to confirm it with the reviewer. My reasons are these: (a) There is a likelihood that this review is a fabrication, and posting it will hopefully lead to a refutation by a legitimate reviewer, (b) If the review is authentic, the new information contained within it that 'Brad' appeared in a porn video could lead to an identification of the escort, (c) Brian's response to the review (see below) is informative. Also, I have received a large volume of messages and emails responding to the alleged picture of 'Brad' and offering their opinions on the identity of 'Brian.' Excerpts from the most relevant and informative of these follow 'Brian's' response.

Brian's response: I had no idea that this client lied to me about his knowledge of Brad's and my history. To say that I'm furious and Brad is devastated is a huge understatement. My agreement with this client to offer medical treatment to Brad in return for sex has been cancelled. From now on, appointments with Brad will be made only after I have administered my quiz in person. Brad has been castrated, and future clients should take that into account. He is depressed, medicated, and in discomfort, and that's just the way it is. Brad claims that he cannot remember if he has ever performed in a porn video. I will confess to you that I lied when I said that the picture on what's-his-fuck's website is not a picture of Brad. I was hoping to keep Brad mysterious, but I realize it's too late for that. That is a picture of the legendary Brad.

Message from ticktock88: I reviewed Brad in September of 2001. To refresh your memory, I picked him up hitchhiking in Northern California. The young man in the picture on sososogreat's homepage is not the young man I reviewed.

Message from anonymous: I know for sure that the guy who's passing himself off as Brian is not who he claims to be. His name is Zack Young. He's a well known figure in the LA barebacking community. I know this because he is a former fuck buddy of mine. We had a huge falling out when Zack date raped and bred (or infected if you prefer) a mutual acquaintance of ours against his wishes. Zack has been making harassing phone calls to me for months. He has bragged that he was behind this Brad and Brian thing ever since I've known him. I think I met Brad, or at least the young man who claims to be Brad, about a month ago. Zack told me at that time that he was Brad and that they had just met a few days before. I didn't believe him until last week when he described the scene described by one of the reviewers where Brad's legs were broken. This was two days before the review appeared. I thought about calling the police but I decided to keep it in the family and tell you what I know instead. I hope you'll post this information on your site so everyone will hear the truth and so that Zack will know that if he tries any revenge number on me everyone will know about it. Thanks.

Message from terencetryst: I live in Portland. I picked Brad up at a hustler bar about seven weeks ago. He told me (and I believed him) that he had recently gotten out of prison, was newly married, and that his pregnant wife had thrown him out after a fight. I put two and two together and realized he was the same Brad whom so many people have written about on this site. I let him stay at my house for a few days. I've looked at the picture that reviewer took and it's not a picture of Brad I've heard through the grapevine that Brad reconciled with his wife and is living here in Portland.

Message from pppeter: I have compared the new picture of Brad to the picture of Brad that was published in the Portland Oregonian. The older picture is of very poor quality, but it's obvious even to the naked eye that these are pictures of two different people.

Review #8

Escort's name: Brad
Location: West Hollywood
Age: 18
Month and year of your date: May 2002
Where did you find him? here
Internet address: no

Escort's email address: meetalegend@hotmail.com

Escort's advertised phone number: 323-660-6555

Rates: $4000/3 hours/4 dudes

Did he live up to his physical description: sure, why not?

Did he live up to what he promised? fucking A

Height: 5'11"

Weight: 135 lbs.

Facial hair: no

Body hair: no

Hair color: pretty long blond chick hair

Eye color: hazel

Dick size: about 6

Thickness: average

Does he smoke? I don't know

Top, bottom, versatile: bottom

In calls/out calls/not sure: in

Kisser: shit, yeah

Has he been reviewed before? yes

Rating: killer

Hire again: yes

Handle: tuff4eal

Submissions: none before

URL for pics: http://hometown.aol.com/userpage/davidbriggs

Experience: Check this out. I've been into Brad since the very old days. I turned some buds onto his shit and we've been chafing for that faggot ever since. This is some seriously primal shit, right? I'm straight as a rule, but I like to get tweaked on the weekends with my buds and raid the faggot bars. We're a hot looking crew that's your average faggot's wet dream, so we pull some pretty max tricks. I'm just saying the shit going down around Brad made heavy changes in my head. I got to know myself deep. It's been a cool ride. I have to say it was crazier than shit to get a look at the fucker after all of that build. I figured he's got to be hot to get that buzz, but that bitch in that picture had some beauty going on. My buds and I were on the same page about getting us some of that shit. I called that Brian freak and tried to work out a deal. We were looking to take Brad off property for some joy riding, gay bashing fun. He was having none of it. I told him, let me email you a picture of my buds and me. I have this bud Hector who's like the sweetest fucking chick you ever saw. Oh yeah, Brian calls me back wanting a piece of that pretty young shit. Hector is a stupid faggot bitch who does exactly what we tell him. So Brian worked it out where he's with Hector and we get to bash Brad. We walk in the door and Brian clocks Hector. I'm talking lights out. We were looking at each other like, damn, this is one serious motherfucker. So we're turned on by that shit and feeling rowdy. Brian tells us how to find the bedroom. Oh shit, let me tell you something real. That fucked up bitch Brad is lying there bare ass naked and it's one sick scene. His face is all beat to hell. He's down with pneumonia or the flu or some shit. We were seriously pissed off. We fucked that sad assed cunt and jizzed his hole. It was three or whatever the hell in the morning. We were like, this is bullshit. We went looking for that Brian freak. He was having it off with our bud, and we were like, Get the fuck off him. We were screaming. He was all apologetic and shit. He gave us back our money. He brought out his stash and got us high, and things were chill. So he says, let's bash your bud Hector then you write in your review that it was Brad. We told him how we had long since had Hector's total, but he could knock himself out and we'll watch. Listen, that freak was serious about getting some of Hector's ass. He was eating out that bitch like it was movie star pussy. Hector's squealing like a chick in love and looking very fresh. So we took a little taste of that shit. Listen, you learn something everyday. One of my buds was like, I think we've been underestimating this bitch. Brian was like, listen, you guys want to taste something nice? You want to taste the fucking sugar? Oh yeah, we were back in that bedroom so fast. Eating out Brad was the killer thing for real. It got our heads back into the whole fucking thing at the beginning. We bashed that famous piece of shit, and gangbanged him to hell, and it was sweet. We jizzed his pretty ass deep down. It's fucking daylight by then. We come out and find that Brian freak all fucking covered with blood. He's raped and beat that pretty bitch Hector so dead we had to carry him out and dump him in a bin behind the Walmart near my mother's house. All and all, it was some experience.

You: Hispanic, 22, tight, hung, built, horny all the time.

Brian's response: I guess it's time for a reality check. Okay, I'm not Brian, or maybe I should say I'm not the original Brian. My name is Zack Young. Some of you will remember me as 'thegayjournalist' who posted on the Brad message board under a number of guises. I was hoping to convince you that I was the original Brian, not for my own sake but for your sake. I thought it would add some myth and weight and pizzazz to Brad's return. The fact is, it doesn't really matter whether I'm the real the original Brian or not. I might as well be the original Brian. It's the same deal. My relationship with Brad is identical. He wants to die. He has given me the power of life and death. I'm sharing the power with you for a reasonable price. I hope this confession will stop all this nattering bullshit around who Brad and I really are so we can get back to the matter at hand. I don't know the story on these guys who are claiming Brad isn't Brad, but I'm telling you the God's honest truth: he is Brad. I went to incredible lengths to get him for you. I got his address in Portland from the real, original Brian. I wrote to him under the guise of Brian asking him to reconcile with me. He responded very positively. We exchanged a number of letters and faxes arranging our reunion. Towards the end of this exchange, I revealed that I wasn't really Brian. Brad's response was that he didn't give a shit whether I was Brian or not. He said he never gave a fuck about Brian. He worked

Brian to get what he wanted and he was happy to work me. The point is, Brad doesn't care that I'm not the original Brian, so why should you? Let's get on with it. This is a monumental, once in a lifetime offer. Do you not understand that? Don't you realize what I'm giving you? Brad isn't just some cute, masochistic piece of ass who's here to help a bunch of stupid leather men gets their sadistic rocks off. He's a fucking legend. I expect you show some respect. Where are the true, devoted Brad fans? If it's a matter of money, we'll work something out. It's far more important to Brad and me that your dates with him mean something important to everyone involved than we make a nice chunk of change. Time is running out, guys. Brad has already taken an irreversible downward turn. It's now or never.

Message from builtlikeatruck44: I've been away from this website for a while and only just checked back in yesterday to discover this new thread of reviews. For those of you who are interested, my company is back in business and things are going very well. If you live in Portland and need some construction work done, I hope you'll think of us. We have a new website if you're interested at www.tonyvillani.com. I have a couple of things to tell you. First of all, the picture of 'Brad' on sososogreat's homepage is not a picture of Brad. The young man in the picture does look vaguely familiar to me. I've been wracking my brains but I can't put my finger on why. I'll keep thinking about it and let you know if my memory is jogged. Brad is fine, as far as I know. He's doing very well, in fact. He lives on the outskirts of Portland with his wife. Or I should say, that was the situation when I spoke to him about two weeks ago. As one of the few people who actually knows Brad, I think I can debunk this new 'Brad' with some authority.

Message from bennybbbixy: I understand there has been some talk and speculation on this website about an amateur gay video called 'Portland Barebackin': Off the Streets.' I am the producer and director of this video. If it helps, I can confirm that the young man in the picture identified as Brad on sososogreat's homepage was one of the performers in this video. I knew him as Thad. Whether that was his real name or not, I can't tell you. The video features five street kids I found in a local hustler bar called The Red Queen. All I can tell you about Thad is that he was a drug addict who told me he grew up in Los Angeles. I knew him for all of three hours. Like most street kids, he talked a lot of crap about how he was going to be rich and famous, and I didn't pay much attention. When the time came to shoot his scene, he was a good performer and that's all I remember. I haven't seen him since and I wouldn't be able to tell you how or why he got mixed up in this nonsense. For those of you who have ordered the video, understand that I wasn't prepared for the recent spike in interest. The video is out of stock, but I'm making new copies, and orders will be filled as quickly as I can. Many of you have called and emailed me to ask if there is unreleased footage or outtakes of Thad from this video shoot. I'm afraid there isn't, but I've recently seen some video footage of Thad having sex with a local john named Albert. The video was shot by the john during their date. It is of very unprofessional quality. Due to the huge interest in Thad, I've reached an agreement with Albert to distribute copies of this video. The video is 85 minutes in length. In the first part of the video, Thad sucks the john's cock and takes a load in his mouth. There is a break in the sex long enough for Thad to do drugs. In the second part, the john rims Thad, fucks him raw, and fist fucks him. There's an anal cum shot and some brief post-orgasm fucking. I hope to be able to ship copies of this video, which I'm calling 'Portland Barebackin': The Brad Tape,' within two weeks. I'm accepting preorders at my website www.rawandrawer.net.

Message from jimmytaylor: This is a message for Brian. I hope you'll put it on your site. Listen, you lying, stupid prick. Next time I call you, you'd better pick the fuck up. You think I'm full of shit? I'll blow this thing out of the water and you know I can. You want me to go public? You'd better talk to me or it's over.

Review #9

Escort's name: Thad
Location: Portland
Age: 18
Month and year of your date: February/March 2002
Where did you find him? street
Internet address: no
Escort's email address: no
Escort's advertised phone number:
Rates: usually $150
Did he live up to his physical description? yes
Did he live up to what he promised? yes
Height: about 5′11″
Weight: about 160-140 lbs.
Facial hair: no
Body hair: just a little bit
Hair color: dirty blond
Eye color: blue
Dick size: 6″
Cut or uncut: cut
Thickness: slender
Does he smoke? yes
Top, bottom, versatile: bottom
In calls/out calls/not sure: out calls
Kisser: yes
Has he been reviewed before: I believe so

Rating: positive
Hire again: yes
Handle: snaredbyboys
Submissions: this is my tenth
URL for pics: http://hometown.aol.com/userpage/davidbriggs/

Experience: I'm not sure if this review qualifies, but I'll submit it. I was a regular of the escort known here as Brad and known to me as Thad until about eight weeks ago. We hooked up seven different times over about a month. I picked him up in an area of downtown Portland where street hustlers are known to work. I was attracted to him initially because he had a rock musician look and style that I happen to go for. When he got into my car, I was pleasantly surprised by his attractive face, sexy blue eyes, and full, edible lips.

I drove him back to my place. He got high, then we stripped and went to bed. I loved holding and caressing his long, skinny, hairless white body. I'm a top in anal sex, but I'm very oral. I licked him all over and spent a long time rimming his tender, warm ass. He was very passive, but would stroke my hair sometimes to let me know he was enjoying himself. As a bottom he was quiet but excellent. I fucked him condom-free in a number of positions and finally shot a big load on his face. I was very satisfied and gave him a nice tip. After that he would call me twice or three times a week asking if I wanted to hook up, and I usually did. I tried to get to know him, but he was reluctant to talk about himself. His favorite line about himself was, 'I'm doomed.' Whenever I asked what that meant, he would get defensive and say he didn't want to talk about it. Eventually I stopped asking.

By about our third date, I noticed Thad was losing weight and seemed to care less and less about his physical appearance. I asked if his health was okay, and he said something like, 'No, but it's not what you're thinking.' The last time I saw him, he seemed different and more optimistic. He was much more affectionate during sex and even cracked a smile once in a while. I asked him why he seemed so happy, and he said something like, 'Because I'm going to be famous soon.' I said something like, 'So you're not doomed anymore.' He started laughing and said, 'Dude, I am so doomed,' like it was a good thing.

I didn't hear from Thad again after that night, and I haven't seen him around since. A guy I know who also tricked with Thad told me there was a picture of him online and mentioned the controversy going on here. That's definitely a picture of Thad, and I thought you'd like to hear my two cents. I think what's going on here is what Thad probably meant by being famous. It's very sad and disturbing if it has come to this. He doesn't have a whole lot going on as a person, but he's a nice and very attractive young man.

You: Just an average guy.

Webmaster's message: I confirmed this review with snaredbyboys. I was unable to confirm the review with Brad/Thad due to the fact that Zack/Brian will not allow me to speak to him. Since confirming these reviews is becoming more difficult, I'm going to do my best to authenticate them. If they appear here, you can assume that I've either confirmed them to my satisfaction or decided to trust my instincts. I continue to receive a huge volume of emails about this thread of reviews. I will post relevant excerpts from the most informative and thought provoking of them as they arrive.

Zack's response: I want everyone to know that I am being blackmailed by the escort Jimmy Taylor. He's threatening to speak a bunch of lies about Brad if I don't pay him an absurd amount of money. I refuse to give in to this petty criminal and liar. I told him that if he wants to hook up, I'd be willing to pay him handsomely for sex. I think this is more than generous of me considering the shit he is pulling. So far he has refused my offer. I want to make all this public so that you'll understand that if he does go through with his threat to 'expose' Brad, he has no credibility whatsoever.

Message from waynebaxter: I want to comment on what Zack or Brian said in his most recent response. I'm talking about his complaints that reviewers aren't expressing enough appreciation of the service he is providing. I have a challenge for him. If you really feel the way you say you do, I wonder if you would accomodate clients who want to rescue Brad. I can only speak for myself, but I can't be the only guy who is drawn to Brad not because we fantasize about torturing or killing him but because we fantasize about saving him from the likes of you. I would argue that the guys who most appreciate Brad are the guys who feel the way I do. You say that you would be willing to reduce Brad's fee if someone was a true 'fan' and showed Brad the proper 'respect.' I don't have much money, but I am a true fan and I do respect Brad. How much would you charge me to take Brad away from you? My fantasy is to do just that, get him treatment for his wounds and emotional problems, and find him a stable and loving home environment. How much, Zack?

Message from builtlikeatruck44: I spoke to Brad on the phone yesterday and told him what was being propagated here in his name. He says he is trying to start a new life and doesn't want to think about his former life. I urged him to look at the reviews and send in a response just to clear up the confusion, and he said he would think about it. In the meantime, I have remembered why the boy in the picture looks familiar. I had sex with him once maybe five months ago. It wasn't a very memorable encounter, which is why I forgot about it. Now that I know who he is, I'm going to query some boys and johns I know in the Portland hustler scene to see if any of them can pass along any helpful information. I'll send in a report if anything comes of this.

Message from snazzystocky: Is it just me, or has the fun and eroticism and intrigue gone out of this Brad thing? I remember the old Brad reviews being so much sexier and more mind blowing. Maybe it's because, as far I can tell, these reviewers are actually doing these things to him and not just making up evil fantasies about him and pretending they're true. I'm a member of the killnickcarter group on Yahoo, and I swear what's going on there is a lot more fun than what's going on here. It's just a lot sexier to read about some guy breaking every bone in Nick Carter's body and tying him into a pretzel, for example, than to read these ugly accounts of cutting Brad's balls off or whatever. Maybe if there were pictures, it would be different. I just think this whole thing has gotten really grim and depressing. I guess I just feel really disappointed. I don't how I expected it to end, but this isn't doing it for me.

Review #10

Escort's name: Brad
Location: West Hollywood
Age: 18
Month and year of your date: May 2002
Where did you find him? here
Internet address: no

Escort's email address: don't know

Escort's advertised phone number: 323-660-6555

Rates: $5000/2 hrs

Did he live up to his physical description? yes

Did he live up to what he promised? yes

Height: 5′11″

Weight: slim

Facial hair: no

Body hair: minimal

Hair color: blond

Eye color: hazel

Dick size: small

Cut or uncut: cut

Thickness: no

Does he smoke? don't know

Top, bottom, versatile: bottom

In calls/out calls/not sure: in call

Kisser: don't know

Has he been reviewed before? yes

Rating: great

Hire again: no

Handle: thebasher

Submission: none before

URL for pics: http://hometown.aol.com/userpage/davidbriggs/

Experience: I'm an S&M master and expert sadist into doling out punishment to young twinks. I've followed this Brad thing with interest and skepticism. I'm used to twinks who say they have no limits then cry for their mamas five minutes into a scene. I'm always on the hunt for a twink who can handle me. Brad seemed like a real possibility, but the smokescreen of bullshit around him made me wonder what was real. When that tasty picture of him showed up online, I decided to take a chance and make an appointment.

Brad's handler claimed that I could inflict heavy, permanent damage on the twink. But the guy has claimed a lot of things that turned out not to be true. When I saw the damage other guys had inflicted on the twink (broken legs, castration, black eye, etc), I felt hopeful. Objectively, I have to say there are hotter twinks in the world, but Brad's charisma more than makes up for it. He has a cute face and a fine ass. His body is sub-twink: pale, thin, no muscle tone, very used looking. I liked him a whole helluva lot, but you vanilla guys should know that he's no porn star. So far so good, but it wasn't until the scene was underway and he was taking heavy punishment that I got what all the hype was about.

To say Brad spoiled me is putting it mildly. He handled a cruel and very hot manual strangulation scene that nearly did him in. I shredded and bloodied his bony back with a series of whips while fucking him hard and deep. His voice really came alive when he was yelling and screaming. I love hearing pain, and he let loose in a big way, which really fired me up. Cock and ball torture is my specialty, and I took most of my aggression out on his lonely, pathetic worm of a cock. I clipped electrodes to the shaft and head and sent jolts through the twink while he bucked and seized in his restraints. I whipped his cock bloody then slowly burned every inch of it with a cigarette lighter until he finally passed out. That did the trick for me, and I shot the biggest load of my life on his slack pussy face.

You: I'm a bigwig in the LA leather community for my perfect body and skill with the whip. I'm 61, but don't look it.

Webmaster's message: I have received some extremely interesting emails as you will see below. I'll let them speak for themselves.

Zack's response: I want to say something about the criticism that Brad and I have been receiving here. You need to understand a few things. Maybe I should have made myself clear earlier. One way that I'm different than the original Brian is that what I'm letting you guys do to Brad is not my fantasy. It's your fantasy, and I just have a sick enough imagination to love observing you. I think you're all assuming I'm in control of this and that Brad is my helpless captive or something. The truth is that Brad wants this to happen. This was his idea. I'm helping his and your fantasy become reality, period. My thing was and is bareback sex—breeding, bug chasing, and so on. Yeah, I like the 'I might be sentencing someone to death when I cum inside him' thing a lot. I love the gambling aspect of raw sex. I love the idea that having hot sex with a bottom could have a permanent, negative impact on his life. I love how barebacking makes having sex heavy and meaningful. I love how gay guys can be like straight guys who wonder how many illegitimate kids there could be out there with their DNA. I love imagining my ex-fucks out in the world infecting others or dying in hospital beds. Honestly, when I hunted Brad down and convinced him to hook up with me, I didn't know what was going to happen. I thought I might fuck him once or a few times and say adios. I thought maybe I could pimp him out to the bareback community and get my rocks off plus earn some money at the same time. It was Brad's idea to go this way and sell pieces of his death. He's the one who wants to die in a big, meaningful, earth shattering way. I'm doing this because it's intense and interesting. I'm doing this because I like the fact that I'm part of something legendary. I like the fame aspect. But if you think I'm here jacking off while guys torture Brad, you're wrong. I have to live with Brad's pain and misery. I have to nurse his wounds and pay for his medical treatment and listen to him moan and cry and whine about his pain and discomfort. I want to know why the fuck he's doing this to himself as much as you do. You think I understand it? I don't. He won't or can't tell me. Maybe I would understand or wouldn't care if I understood if I actually gave a shit about him. I don't. There's nothing to care about. We had some very hot sex when he first got here. He had a cute face. He had a cute little ass. But the sex was hot because it was intense to be fucking a boy I'd been obsessing about for so long. Apart from that, I didn't think he was interesting or sweet or fun or intriguing or even all that physically attractive. What was and is missing is the love. Brad clearly never loved Brian. He's too massively self-absorbed to feel anything for anyone else. But Brian loved Brad, or always said he did. I can't for the life of me figure out why, but he obviously did. I've been trying to get in touch with the original Brian to get some advice or understanding, but he won't respond to my emails. I'm so desperate to understand that I was willing to pay that nasty little piece of shit whore Jimmy Taylor an insane amount of money for sex just so I could talk to someone who knew Brad even superficially. The point is, you've got it all wrong. I'm not like you.

Zack's response part 2: I got so overwrought in my first response that I forgot to tell you why I was writing in the first place. Brad has some major appointments scheduled in the next two weeks. Those of you who want to meet with him should mark these dates on your calendars and plan accordingly. Tomorrow, Brad's penis will be amputated. the-basher's damage to Brad's penis was severe. I've been advised that this operation is necessary to prevent infection and to allow Brad to urinate properly. Also know that the following body parts have been reserved and are likely to be heavily damaged. This Sunday, his face. Next Tuesday, his arms will be amputated at the shoulders. Next Thursday, his ass. A week from this coming Wednesday, all of this will be over. Those of you who want to have conventional sex with Brad should make appointments ASAP. As I mentioned before, if you're a big fan and can prove it, we'll work out a fee that's fair to us and reasonable for you. If you're young (18-22), versatile or a bottom, cute, smooth, slender, and interested in hooking up with me as well, I'll consider making your date with Brad a freebie. Guys, the end is in sight. It's now or never.

Message from Brad: My name is Brad Gordon. My friend Tony Villani told me to check out this website and read the reviews for Brad in the Los Angeles section. It doesn't seem like you're talking about me, but Tony says you are. He told me that I should tell you these reviews aren't about me but it seems like you already know that. When I was living in LA last year and going through some bad shit I did prostitution for a while. I lived at a man named Brian's house for a while. I think he's the Brian you're talking about. He was sort of my pimp and I guess I can say we were a couple. I thought he was a funny man and intelligent. We had fun pranking some of the men who had dates with me but now it seems really uncool that we did that. Brian turned out be kind of a major creep. He was always making jokes about how he thought it would be sexy to kill me. I didn't think he was serious until he tried to kill me. I took off for Portland after that. When I got here, I did prostitution for a while and things got really fucked up and I ended up in prison for a few months. After my release, I got married. My wife and I have a little daughter. I'm working for a construction company right now but I'm hoping to save up some money and open a crafts store with my wife. I'm not saying things are perfect for me. My wife and I fight sometimes. I've slipped and done a couple of tricks one time when she threw me out of our house, but we're doing a lot better now. It's hard for me to think about my old life because I'm trying to be different now. It just makes me feel guilty about some things I did that weren't so nice. About a few months ago, this guy I used to run around with when I was doing prostitution up here told me I got an email from that man Brian at an old address of mine that I let him use. He read it to me, and I told him that it didn't sound like Brian, and even if it was him, I didn't want to have anything to do with him. I told my wife about it and she confessed that she and some other prostitute guys I used to know had pulled some kind of scam about me and that man Brian. I didn't really understand what she was talking about. She said that when I was in prison, she and these guys had pretended to be me to get money. I thought it was a bunch of bullshit and I guess I didn't believe her. When Tony told me about all the stuff going on this website, I called the guy who read me the email and asked whatever happened with that. He said he'd thought about scamming some money off of Brian by pretending to be me but he changed his mind and let this friend of his who's also a prostitute do the scam. His friend's name is Thad. I used to know him a little, but I didn't like him very much. I think you guys are talking about Thad but I think you know that already. I never knew Thad very well. He was much more hardcore into prostitution than I was and we didn't have much in common. I was only a prostitute for a few months, and I never liked it. I think I just did it because I was broke and I wanted a father figure in my life. The only good thing about it was that I met Tony and he's kind of a father figure to me and a really nice guy even though I did something really bad to him when I first knew him. Brian was just a man I knew for a while in Los Angeles. We were never a serious couple or in love or anything like that. I've hardly thought about him since the last time I saw him except when people mention him to me. My life is really different now. I can't relate to all of this stuff you guys are talking about. I never wanted to die. I did S&M a couple of times when I was a prostitute, but I didn't like it. People say I'm good looking and I think I'm a nice guy most of the time but I'm not really at that special. Nobody except for my wife and Tony ever made me feel like I was special. I don't know why you guys are obsessed with me but you don't know me at all, and I think you should get a life.

Message from builtlikeatruck44: I've discovered a wealth of information about the escort Thad. I think I can say with certainty that he's the young man who is masquerading as Brad. This information comes courtesy of a street hustler here in Portland named Trent who is Thad's best friend. He's in possession of Thad's belongings and allowed me to look through them. Thad's full name is Thaddeus Stroh. His parents are first generation German Americans. He's 20 years old and grew up in Alhambra, California. He moved to Portland to attend a local university but developed serious depression and dropped out after one semester. He stayed in Portland and developed a drug habit, then started hustling to pay for drugs. When Trent met him, he was having blackouts and migraines. Trent talked him into seeing a local doctor who treats street hustlers in return for sex. Thad was diagnosed as having advanced leukemia and was told he would die within in a year. I might add that I know this doctor socially and he confirmed to me that Thad does have terminal leukemia. Trent says that Thad's personality changed after that. He became very self-destructive and didn't give a shit about anything. He started having unsafe sex and would let men beat him up or urinate and defecate on him for money. One of his tricks introduced him to the Brad and Brian discussion on this website, and Trent says Thad became completely obsessed with Brad and talked about him constantly. He told Trent that he completely related to Brad because he was also dying and wanted to go out with a bang. He buddied up to some local hustlers who knew Brad and started hanging out with them. Trent says Thad was really disappointed when he finally met Brad. He thought Brad was a poseur and boring. He told Trent that he needed to meet Brian because he was better than Brad, and they would be perfect for each other. He would go into internet cafes and post messages on the old Brad and Brian message board hoping to make contact with Brian, but Trent doesn't know what these messages entailed. Trent said Thad's health started declining really fast and he started looking terrible and talking crazily. He says that around that time, one of Brad's friends told him he had gotten an email for Brad from Brian. Thad begged to read the email and write back to Brian, and the guy agreed. Trent says Thad wrote back and forth with Brian pretending to be Brad, and then left his belongings with Trent one day and took off for LA supposedly to be with him. Trent says Thad was acting strangely happy and upbeat the last time they saw each other. Thad told Trent that he had changed his name to Brad and told him to look for things about Brad and Brian on this website. Trent says he read the first few recent Brad reviews and it made him feel so depressed that he stopped looking at this website. I thought you'd find this very enlightening.

Message from jimmytaylor: Never trust a whore. Didn't your mothers ever tell you that?! I'm proud of this one. I just got back from seeing that prick Zack. What a loser. He tries to come off all evil genius but he's just a gay clone asshole into screwing young street trade. He's no better than every other gay idiot I've ever tricked with, and he's worse than some of them. I'd told him on the phone if he gave me $3000 I'd shut up about Brad and his little bullshit scheme. I would have done what I promised if he didn't make screwing me part of the deal. The minute he sees me he says he wants to screw me too. When gay guys pull shit like that on me, I don't think I owe them anything. I think taking his AIDS cum up my ass is worth more than $3000 easily. So after he fucks the shit out of me, he tells me I'm lying about his whore not being Brad. I tell him, Oh yeah, prove it. Show me Brad. He refuses because he knows full fucking well that whoever he's trying to pass as Brad isn't Brad. I say, Fuck you, I'm going to look for myself, and the fucker pulls a gun on me and tells me he'll shoot me if I don't leave right now. I said, Brad's living in Portland with his fucking wife, you asshole, but thanks for the $3000. Later. I have to say the guy has a nice scam going on. Props to him about that. I almost feel bad about blowing his shit out of the water, but not really.

Review #11

Escort's name: Thad?
Location: West Hollywood
Age: 18

Month and year of your date: May 2002

Where did you find him: this website

Internet address: unknown

Escort's email address: unknown

Escort's advertised phone number: 323-660-6555

Rates: $2500/hr

Did he live up to his physical description? not if you want Brad

Did he live up to what he promised? he did, Zack Young didn't

Height: about 5′11″

Weight: thin

Facial hair: none

Body hair: none

Hair color: blond

Eye color: hazel

Dick size: 6 inches

Cut or uncut: cut

Thickness: unknown

Does he smoke? no

Top, bottom, versatile: bottom

In calls/out calls/not sure: in calls

Kisser: unknown

Has he been reviewed before? yes

Rating: disturbing

Hire again: no

Handle: godsrighthand

Submissions: none

URL for pics: http://hometown.aol.com/userpage/davidbriggs/

Experience: I intended to submit a very different and glowing review. After reading the previous review and responses, I just feel duped and angry and sick to my stomach. I set up my date and paid a ridiculously high fee in the belief that I would be with Brad. Obviously, I was mislead. If prostitution were legal, I would sue Zack Young for everything he's worth. All I can do now is add my voice to the chorus of attacks on these swindlers and pray to God for His divine forgiveness.

I paid to damage Brad's face to the point of no return. I paid to destroy the face that launched countless depraved, Godless fantasies and lonely, depressing orgasms. I didn't pay to torture and maim the face of some lying, self-hating piece of Portland trash Zack Young offered me the greatest moment of my life and then sold me a lifetime of guilt. I can only pray that the boy does have terminal leukemia. That would be my only comfort and salvation.

Excuse me if I don't go into great detail about my experience, but the memory is too painful. The basics are as follows. After paying Zack Young, he introduced me to the boy I believed was Brad. The boy was lying heavily sedated on his back in a bed fitted with a rubber sheet. His legs were in casts and his crotch was bandaged from the two operations already reported here. His body was very thin and bruised, and his face had the look of having been in a recent fistfight. Overall, I thought he was an appealing shadow of someone who obviously had been very attractive. Had I known he wasn't Brad, I'm not sure I would have given him the benefit of a doubt.

While I undressed, Zack Young sat the boy up, tied his hands behind his back, and laid him down again. I straddled his chest and looked at him intently for a moment, recalling everything I believed that I knew about him. When I was ready, I grabbed a fistful of his long, dirty hair and started punching him as hard as I could in the face. I'm a big, strong guy and former boxer who knows how to hit. My third or fourth punch knocked the boy out. I kept punching until his nose and front teeth broke, his lips and right eyebrow split open, and cuts opened on his cheeks and forehead. I put my hand inside his mouth and pushed down with all my strength until his jaw broke. Then I punched him in the eyes until they were swollen shut, and threw another round of general punches until Zack Young stopped me for fear that I would accidentally kill the boy. I finished off by rolling him over and raping his ass until I shot my load inside him.

This was supposed to be the greatest moment of my life and the worst moment of Brad's life. I would never have done that to someone I didn't even know. I'm not interested in assisting the suicide of some cancer victim. I don't know how I feel about that morally. I was never given the chance to make a moral decision. Zack Young's deceit has turned me into someone I'm not. I wanted a heavy experience, not to have my life changed forever. Consider this review a warning to everyone out there who wants to play a part in Brad's story.

You: A man with a shattered dream.

Zack's response: For the record, I didn't know or at least wouldn't let myself believe that my Brad wasn't the real Brad until the incident described by Jimmy Taylor in his recent message. Brad's history is built on myths and lies, some of which I admit to perpetrating myself. So when people claiming to be former clients of Brad started claiming that my Brad wasn't Brad, I couldn't take these claims seriously. You feel ripped off? How do you think I feel? I've been living a lie too. When this kid Thad first scammed me into believing he was Brad, I found it difficult to believe that such a wasted, moderately cute lowlife kid could have inspired so much devotion and gossip. But I took Thad at his word because he knew so much about Brad and I guess I just wanted to believe it. All of this became clear the afternoon of godsrighthand's date, and I admit I didn't tell him the truth. I was still in shock at that point. While I don't feel responsible for what has happened, I do want to apologize for ruining the experiences which some of you have treasured by revealing the truth to you now. If my hand hadn't been forced, I would have continued to let you believe Thad was Brad for everyone's sake. It's too late now. The scandal is too big to reverse with lies, however clever. All I can do is tell you where we are right now and inform you of a drastic change in the future of this enterprise. Until a few days ago, I had twelve confirmed appointments for next week. Eleven of these appointments have now been cancelled by the clients. The only client who has no problem with Brad being an imposter is the guy who had an appointment to end this whole thing once and for all. I'm sure there's something deep and meaningful in the fact that the killer is the only one who doesn't care, but I'll leave you to ponder. I've moved that client's appointment up to tonight. I doubt you'll hear from me again.

Message from Brian: This is Brian, aka the real Brian, as much as there has ever been a Brian, since that's not my real name. But then I doubt there has been more than one or two real names given throughout this whole ridiculous shebang. You get my point. I'm the same guy you've been talking and speculating and lying about for so long. Originally, I wasn't going to reenter the fray. I was going to leave you to finish what I started in your own strange way and just read the goings on from the sidelines. But when I saw Brad's message, I thought I might as well say hello too. What Brad told you about him and me is the truth. We were never in love. We never even liked each other. I was an evil, heartless creep to him, and he was an evil, heartless creep to me. It's taken me a long time to realize that. I haven't changed much, and I doubt he has either. I was obsessed with him for a long time, and he was into being the object of my obsession for about three months. I tried to kill him, and he didn't want to be killed. He lost interest in me at that moment, and I eventually lost interest in him. I have a cute, fucked up mess of a young boyfriend now who thinks he loves me. I don't think I love him, but then I don't think I love anyone. It might work out, or we might break up someday, or I might kill him. Brad's marriage might work out, or he might end up back on the streets, or someone might kill him for whatever reason. Yes, I gave Zack Brad's email address, but I knew Brad didn't use it anymore. The fact that some kid co-opted it to do a number on Zack was news to me, but then nothing about this thing really surprises me. Since then, I haven't been here. I've just been reading about 'us' like you. For what it's worth, I think this whole thing has turned grim and unimaginative. Everyone seems to want this to end in some logical way. I started this whole thing because I wanted to know and feel something important, and when I eventually realized it wouldn't happen with Brad, I gave up. Of course I knew Brad, and you didn't. Brad was just your idea, and I guess you think he's a great idea. He may be a great idea, but Brad himself is just a kid who got drafted into the job of representing an idea. Now Brad is just a name. You don't even know who it belongs to anymore. The point is, this is your story and your ending, not Brad's and mine. I used to wish our story would end something like this. Maybe I still wish it had, but it didn't and it won't.

Review #12

Escort's name: Thad?

Location: West Hollywood

Age: 18

Month and year of your date: May 2002

Where did you find him?

Internet address:

Escort's email address:

Escort's advertised phone number:

Rates:

Did he live up to his physical description? yeah

Did he live up to what he promised? yeah

Height: medium

Weight: scrawny

Facial hair: unknown

Body hair: none

Hair color: blond?

Eye color: hazel?

Dick size: none

Cut or uncut: none

Thickness: none

Does he smoke? no

Top, bottom, versatile: bottom

In calls/out calls/not sure: in

Kisser: no

Has he been reviewed before? yes

Rating: perfect
Hire again:
Handle:
Submissions:
URL for pics:

Experience: I'm writing this review because I don't want to be a spoilsport. I feel a lot of pressure to say something profound. I feel like everyone reading this has huge expectations. I'm telling you right now this was about me and the escort. I don't care who he was or wasn't.

I see cute young boys everywhere. I hate that I can't fuck them. I hire escorts, but I hate them too. They act like their asses are the cure for cancer or something. They're never as cute as the boys I want. There's always something wrong and third rate about them.

A friend told me about this escort. I read his reviews and linked to his picture. I thought he was cute as far as escorts go. If I saw him in a gay bar, I would have thought he was a skank. I hated that I wanted him. I hated that his reviewers gave him so much credit.

I called Zack. We met at a bar so he would know I was legitimate. After I ranted about how I hate escorts, he was convinced. He gave me a price and an appointment two weeks from then. A few days later, he called me and asked if I wanted to do it now.

The escort was all beat to hell and drugged. He still had

a nice ass. I fucked him raw. He didn't react at all. I brought a handgun with me. When I was angry enough, I shot him in the back of the head. I shot him again in the mouth to make sure. Then I jacked off on his ass.

I'd agreed to get rid of the body. Zack helped me wash it off. We put it in my trunk. I asked if I could use the bathroom. When we got back inside the house, I shot Zack in the head. I did that because I knew he could identify me. I didn't hate him.

I put the bloody bedding and towels in my trunk. I drove somewhere and burned the escort's body. I also burned the bedding, the towels, and my clothes. I drove home and started writing this before I go to bed. The only thing profound is that I feel great.

You:

Webmaster's message: I received this review five days ago. I immediately attempted to contact Zack Young, and was unable to do so. At that point, I made a decision to phone the police. They discovered Zack Young dead from a single gunshot wound to the head. The police have asked me to turn over all postings, emails, and reviews that might prove to have some relevance to Zack Young's death, and I have done so. They requested that I post this review in the hopes that it might lead to tips from readers of this website. However, based on the evidence found thus far, Zack Young's death has been ruled a suicide. No evidence has been found to suggest that there is a second victim or that anyone other than Zack Young has been living in his house during the past six months.

Webmaster's follow-up message: Because of the chaos surrounding Zack Young's death, I neglected to read my incoming emails for the past week. This morning I checked my emails and found the following email from Zack Young. It was sent on May 29, 2002.

Dear Webmaster,

I need to clear my conscience. I've been lying to you and to everyone who reads this website. I maintained the lie for as long as I could but I don't have it in me to keep going. I don't have the imagination to pull this off. I realized that today and made a decision to come clean to you because either way I lose.

The truth is I started this in good faith. I went to great effort to get Brad for you and finish this thing off right. He wasn't Brad. He sure fooled me for a while, but I know how easy it is to bullshit someone when you know what he wants to hear. The first six reviews were real. After that, the Brad imposter fucked me over and left. I wrote the rest of the reviews except for the review of 'Thad' from the guy in Portland.

Brad or Thad or whoever lied to me and maybe to himself

that he could die for glory. At least I know that the same thing happened to Brian, which is some consolation. But after reviewer #4 broke my boy's legs, he changed his mind. He wanted to leave, but I wouldn't let him. One day when I got home from buying groceries, he was gone. Someone must have helped him leave, but I don't know who. I just hope the little prick does have leukemia and suffers a long, miserable death.

I'll be honest with you. Whoever the boy was, Brad or Thad or someone else, he wasn't attractive or interesting or good enough in the sack to have lived up to the hype even if he had let himself be killed. From reading that email from the supposed real Brad, I doubt he was either. That's why I ended up thinking it was better if there wasn't a Brad at all. Not that I had a choice. After reviewer #5 posted that picture, and everyone grew suspicious that he wasn't Brad, the appointments had dried up anyway.

I'm a pretty great liar, so I started writing fake reviews. I thought I could make up a better ending than whatever would have happened anyway. But too many questions were raised by too many people. I had to keep addressing them to make the reviews seem plausible. It just became impossible to satisfy everyone and create the perfect death at the same time.

By the time I wrote the last review earlier tonight, I'd basically given up on the whole thing. I realized it was impossible. Jimmy Taylor had busted me, or at least raised too much suspicion. The postings by Brad and especially

Brian were the clinchers. I wanted to respond to them by thinking up a great fuck you ending, but I'd cornered myself and I was out of my league.

Still, I would like to pull off the last review if I can. I realize it probably won't work. I'm telling you the truth because my conscience is bothering me. But I ask if you would keep this email between you and me, if you don't mind. At least that way people reading these reviews will feel like they got what they wanted even if they aren't happy about how it played out.

Zack Young

About the Author

Dennis Cooper is the author of The George Miles Cycle, an interconnected sequence of five novels (*Closer, Frisk, Try, Guide,* and *Period*) that have been translated into sixteen languages. He is also the author of the novels *My Loose Thread* and *God, Jr.* Cooper has also published a book of stories, *Wrong,* and several volumes of poetry, including *The Dream Police.* He lives in Los Angeles.